A Loud Humming Sound
Came From Above

Johnny Strike

Illustrated By Richard Sala

RUDOS AND RUBES PUBLISHING
A division of Lime Ventures LP
535 Stevenson St.
San Francisco, CA 94103
http://www.rudosandrubes.com

A LOUD HUMMING SOUND CAME FROM ABOVE.
Copyright © 2008 Johnny Strike. All rights reserved. Printed in the U.S.A. No part of this book may be reproduced or transmitted in any form or by any means, electronic or mechanical, without the written permission of the Publisher.
Interior design: Heinz Kremhold and Marie Davenport.

Earlier versions of the following stories appeared in the specified books and publications.

CRAZY CARL'S THING: *Carved in Rock*
(Thunder's Mouth Press, U.S.A., 2003)
NIGHT FLAMERS: Ambit 173 (U.K., 2003)
AS YOU WISH: Ambit 174 (U.K., 2003)
THE HOMELESS MUTANTS: Si Señor, Volume 3 (U.S.A., 2005)
LADY KILLER: Si Señor, Volume 4 (U.S.A., 2006)
JIMMY BALLARD'S HOSPITAL REVIEW: Ballardian.com
(Australia, 2005)

Library of Congress Control Number: 2007928047
Strike, Johnny
          A Loud Humming Sound Came From Above/Johnny Strike
Illustrated by Richard Sala

ISBN 978-0-9778952-0-5

Thanks to Martin Bax, Gregory Ego, Alice Lienkiwicz, Kenneth Lisenbee, Francisco de Oliveira Mattos, Peter Maravelis, Michael O'Connor, Simon Sellars, and Diane Senechal. Special thanks to Karen Asbelle.

Dedicated to the neglected writers of pulp literature who banged away on manual typewriters deep into the night, coming out the other side with tales of exotica, raw crime, and fantasy—all shot through with the sheer madness of life itself.

The Homeless Mutants	11
A Transaction In Souls	23
As You Wish	35
Night Flamers	51
Other Ports, Other Hells	57
The Girl From Somewhere	75
Mister Leposki	87
Lady Killer	95
Boiled In Miami	105
Jimmy Ballard's Hospital Review	119
Crazy Carl's Thing	141
The Methadone Clinic	149

A Loud Humming Sound Came From Above

The Homeless Mutants

How had Lester become homeless? It seemed that one day he just was. But, of course, it wasn't like that at all. There were significant incidents that led up to it. First, there was the loss of his job. Second, the end of his five-year relationship with Bobby. Depression followed and then the gradual draining of his bank account. Finally, the loss of his apartment. He stayed with friends for a while, then got a room with some money that came in from the sale of his deceased mother's small diamond ring. But one day soon thereafter, he awoke to find that his options had all run out. He spent a rough week at a shelter, then was turned away even from there. He was told he could return in three days but he'd vowed that he would not. It had been a nightmare of disgusting smells, the ever-present possibility of being attacked while asleep, and an uncomfortable cot in a room filled with other men farting, coughing, screaming—and worse.

He was too embarrassed to ask friends for the use of their showers and couches anymore and his appearance was deteriorating to the point where he didn't even want them to see him. There had already been some incidents when he'd spotted people he knew and turned away. He felt he'd never really known desolation and loneliness until now and the streets, the city, and everything about it were frightening. But strangely, he felt more aware of himself, and his senses, although raw, were roused to a higher state now that his basic survival was at stake.

Lester was a budding underground comic artist, and his dream was to create a comic book on his own and sell it to a publisher. Six months before, he'd begun the comic, which ironically he'd called *The Homeless Mutants*. "HOMELESS PEOPLE TURNING INTO MUTANTS," a piece in the *Weekly World News*, had sparked his imagination and he'd decided to use it as a jumping-off point. He still carried the clipping in his wallet. The extravagantly lurid subtitle of the *Weekly* read: "MILLIONS OF STREET DWELLERS MORPHING INTO CREATURES WITH HUGE EYES—AND CLAWS!" Lester had completed only a few panels of preliminary sketches and then couldn't seem to find the time to get back to it. But he hadn't forgotten it, either, and now, at this low point, he began thinking about the comic book again.

The article described the mutants as having developed humped backs from dumpster diving, a dog's acute sense of hearing, tough reptilian skin, and highly-developed immunity to viruses and germs. It had been fun drawing the mutants from the descriptions. He'd had a pack of them slinking through back alleys. Then he'd worked on the startled expressions of pedestrians as they caught a glimpse of them. Of course, Lester had seen no mutants since he'd been on the street, although he did see some frightening human specimens.

The Homeless Mutants

There were some choice characters amongst his new acquaintances who had chosen to hang around the same part of town. Willy, for one, was a man who wore pants to fit a man twice his size and sneakers so large that he looked like a filthy clown bum.

Lee, a Chinese fellow with bushy, black hair, pushed his shopping cart around the block in an endless circle, only resting for a few hours in the morning while leaning on his cart. Lee carried stacks of notebooks that he filled with figures and symbols that only he could decipher. They looked as though they might have had some connection to a lost, ancient language or maybe an extraterrestrial origin, Lester mused. He worked in them while he slowly pushed and steered the cart with his body. He always seemed to be working on some monumental problem. Then again, Lee counted on his fingers, so could he really be working on a level that was all that advanced?

Mr. Dicker, another character, was blind and today Lester spotted him sitting on an abandoned red and white couch on the sidewalk, eating some slop off a paper plate, as content as he would be sitting in his own home. The couch was horribly stained and missing cushions, but its pattern of huge red flowers imbued a festive mood around Mr. Dicker, who was unshaven and chewing a mouthful of mush thoughtfully. A new neighbor, nameless thus far, was a boy with long hair who was wrapped in a blanket, Indian pow wow style, holding out a plastic cup for money.

Today, Lester found an entire box of exceptionally good paper thrown out in an alley. He'd come by some nice pens and pencils the same way at a recent dumpster feast where he'd also scored a pillow and some toothpaste. Now, when the sun came up, he'd go back to "his" spot behind an abandoned building where he would climb up to the landing and draw. Though he could begin the same comic from memory, he now added his daily observations and experiences.

He was fast at work, smoking a hand-rolled cigarette and sipping from a canteen, when he heard a woman's voice.

"Excuse me, young man."

Lester looked down to see a middle-aged woman wearing a thermal parka and a fur-lined hat. She held a clipboard in front of her. That parka would be nice for this weather, Lester was thinking.

"Yeah?"

"Would you like to come tonight and have a big bowl of curry and rice? Even a salad and warm cornbread and real butter?"

The words alone made Lester's mouth water and his stomach growl and grumble as he felt it awaken and demand to be fed. Lester put his drawing aside and came down the few steps to meet this brave humanitarian. She was a tiny woman. She handed him a coupon and had him spell out his last name, which she added to a list on the clipboard.

"Do you know this address?" she asked, pointing to his coupon with her pen.

"Sure do, ma'am. I'll be there at six. Thank you kindly." He had never used "ma'am" before and, to his recollection, had never said "thank you kindly" either. She said goodbye and walked off in search of another

The Homeless Mutants

soul. Again, he was impressed with her fearlessness, wandering these back alleys of skid row.

At six o'clock, Lester arrived at the "Bowl O' Curry Vigil" at the address on the coupon. On the door of the old hall was an orange and white banner: "Homelessness and Hunger Awareness Week."

Inside, Lester was soon nearly swooning over his bowl of curry and rice and chunk of cornbread. The hall was almost filled with other street people sitting at wooden tables and scarfing down the food. In the back were various agencies' booths that offered help and services to the homeless. On a stage, a thin man in suspenders and dark glasses was speaking into a microphone.

"People have an image of what a homeless person should be. I didn't fit any of the descriptions. I came from a wealthy family in Kankakee, Illinois. I attended university in Decatur. But there I discovered alcohol. One day I got a notice that said I had thirty days to move."

The man stopped to take a sip of water. "I was forced to live between motels and friends' homes—and being codependent for my alcoholic girlfriend. I didn't want to live in my car, but that's where I was heading. Then I was approached by some people here, and now I have a job and a room."

Some gathered in the eating party grumbled and others snorted and coughed.

"Scott Henderson," who looked like a construction worker, spoke next. He had grown up in a poor family and had ended up homeless. "I used to be depressed," he said. "And I thought of suicide. Over the

A Loud Humming Sound Came From Above

years, I've been in and out of homelessness, but now I'm a staff worker at a shelter." Henderson stopped to survey his audience.

"So many people don't worry about the future," he scolded. "And there are many people you'd never expect to be homeless who arrive at the shelter."

Yeah, alright already, so what, Lester thought, finishing off his salad.

"One of the common misconceptions about the homeless is that they're too lazy to work," Henderson said. "People need to take into account the possibility that these men and women could have mental or physical disorders that prevent them from obtaining available jobs."

Henderson told the story of a man at the shelter who had "Reflex Sympathetic Dystrophy," which caused muscle deterioration. "Because this disease has not been researched in depth, he wasn't eligible for any disability checks and had to find other ways to pay for treatment. When he couldn't afford the pills, a pharmacist offered him a container with fewer pills for a reduced price, but each pill would cost more." Henderson made a grimace of disgust. "Price gouging is just unacceptable," he said.

"I have seen three homeless deaths in the past year," said "Jake," a wizened old codger. "One of my homeless friends was found frozen behind a dumpster. He crawled between the dumpster and a concrete wall to stay warm. It was twenty below zero that night. He went back there thinking that hot grease from the restaurant was going to be dumped and the heat from the grease would get him warm. But there was no grease that night. They had to scrape his frozen body from the concrete.

"The other death was in the heat of summer," Jake continued. "The man was quite old, and had become homeless after the death of his wife. He carried a bag for his body waste. He used to tell me that he couldn't wait for death, so that he wouldn't be homeless anymore. They found him dead on the steps of a church. He is no longer homeless.

"Another man, one of my best friends, used to sleep on a pad near me. He was a heavy drinker. He said he could get the warmth he needed from the bottle. He would get so drunk that nothing else mattered. He stole to eat, at times. And he got caught for it. But jail was only a place to stay for a night or two. He began sleeping in a homemade tent that he hid near the railroad tracks. Well, one night, he never made it to the tent. He got run over by a train. So I ask you, when will people really help to stop the madness?" Jake had run over his time and was escorted off the stage by one of the staff.

Another staff member, a fat hippie wearing a Nirvana t-shirt, now spoke to the captive and apathetic crowd in the old hall that smelled of stale clothes and curry. It all started to sound like babble to Lester, who was feeling downright drowsy after the meal, but he pretended to listen attentively.

"Homeless here are being banned from places that have been used as camps in the past," the hippie stated. "Granted, there are health concerns, but we're not being given any viable options. The shelters are maxed out. There used to be a car camp every winter

A Loud Humming Sound Came From Above

that had staff from local services onsite and a liaison officer from the police department. Bathrooms and shower facilities were provided. Not anymore. Every night, large buildings all over town with bathroom and kitchen facilities go empty. Community resources are overloaded. And huge churches are empty most of the time, but won't open facilities to the homeless because of insurance, lack of volunteers, expense, liability, etc. There are many large commercial as well as government-owned buildings that are empty, too. It's the season of tragedy, and this winter is looking particularly grim. It feels like we're waiting for a slaughter. It's unimaginable and we're here to try and stop that."

    Although it was warm inside, the talk was starting to bore Lester and give him a slight headache so he got up to leave. He was stopped at the door by different workers wanting him to sign petitions and fill out questionnaires. He told them he was just stepping out for a cigarette and that he'd be right back. Outside, he quickly crossed the street and turned a corner. He leaned at a stoop and lit up a hand-rolled cigarette. The meal had been a godsend. The only other food he'd had all day was an Egg McMuffin, a coffee, and a stolen apple that was too sour for his taste—though he'd eaten it anyway. Now he would go back to his landing, in the hope that someone else hadn't tried to stake a claim. It was a nice spot that got the daytime sun and was partially sheltered from the wind and rain. As he smoked, he noticed a group of men coming down the street toward him. As they approached, he saw that they were Chinese youths wearing over-

The Homeless Mutants

sized rapper or gang-type clothes—Lester had no idea which. They were swaggering and Lester looked away, wanting to avoid any eye contact.

"The fuck you lookin' at, bitch?" one of them taunted, apparently trying to sound gangsta.

Lester still looked away but with escalating dread, knowing that they had stopped.

"Don't fuckin' ignore me, scumbag."

They were all laughing now like sick hyenas. Lester turned to find the four moving from side to side in a menacing dance. Lester looked around frantically: Where was anybody? The street he'd picked to stop on was completely deserted.

"Please, leave me alone," Lester pleaded.

But the four, one by one, flicked open knives that glittered under the light of the street lamps. Lester saw the oft-described life-flash, saw his death, and then something else: climbing down a wall across the dim street were three figures with hunched backs—three deformed ninjas.

"I-I was looking at them," Lester said, staring beyond the thugs at the approaching mutants. Yes, that's what they were: mutants. Their eyes were wide and gave off a pinkish light. Their hands were oversized claws and they were coming for the gang. When the thugs saw them, their expressions of idiot hatred and stupidity turned to confusion, then terror. They began to scream, but their screams were cut short as the mutants were on them slicing and hacking like manic butchers in a sped-up film. The claws were multifunctional: razors, scissors, and cleavers. In moments, they'd begun to feast on the dead flesh. The

19

A Loud Humming Sound Came From Above

leader turned to Lester and gestured that he should go.

Lester walked off as fast as he could, his legs and body still shaking. As he was making his way back to the landing, he spotted Lee coming toward him with his overpacked shopping cart. Lee stopped and stared at Lester, wide-eyed. He pointed to his notebook and then at Lester and started yelling in Chinese. Lester hurried away. Once he made it to his landing, he bundled up and got the cardboard arranged around himself.

Then he heard a shriek and looked out to see the mutant leader crouching near him and smiling. He was holding Lester's sketchbook and nodding appreciatively. Lester found the creature's eyes oddly compelling now. His skin, close up, was like smooth, fine leather.

"Come, Lester," he said gently. "You can be like us. No need to sleep out here like an animal.

"Come, I'll take you Underneath."

A Transaction In Souls

Jackie Grisman glanced at gray water as the plane came in for its landing at SFO. Fog was everywhere and he imagined the plane crashing and how that would take care of everything. But it landed okay despite some rumbles and bumps that made the lady next to him grab her seat handle. He stayed put while passengers stood, grappled with overhead bags, and lined up to wait for their release. He waited till even the stragglers got their extra luggage down and moved off. Then, alone, he left the plane and walked the jetway into the cold terminal.

Jackie went to the baggage carousel and spotted his bag right away. He grabbed it, walked out of the airport and waited in line for a taxi. He got into a Yellow cab and told the driver to take him to the Holiday Inn on Van Ness. The hotel had twenty-six floors and would make a good jump if he lost his nerve to actually do it from the Golden Gate Bridge.

Right before the taxi reached the checkout booth, the driver turned around, grinned, and asked Jackie how he was doing. Jackie thought the guy had a face like a cartoon drawing of a hoodlum. In the rear view mirror, the driver introduced himself as Crazy Tony and laughed in a way that put him on edge. Jackie

A Loud Humming Sound Came From Above

looked out the window, hoping that the cabbie would just shut up and drive. He was considering saying something along those lines when he saw that the ID picture on the visor was not the man driving the cab. After a moment of panic, he calmed himself down.

"Excuse me, driver. Mister Hell-er-man, is it?"

"Yeah?"

"Are you Sidney Hellerman?"

"I could be. What's your name?"

"Jackie A. Grisman."

The driver snorted and looked back at him in the rear view mirror, dark eyes searching and gloating at the same time. Jackie looked away to an empty field as they moved down 101 toward San Francisco. Maybe he was borrowing the cab to make a few extra bucks, Jackie reasoned.

"Why ya wanna go to the Holiday?" the driver asked. "That one is inna very blah neighborhood. Lots of airlines put their crews up there. Been a couple of jumpers there, too. Is it the price?"

Was this guy psychic? Jackie wondered. Or was his mention of jumpers only a coincidence?

"Listen, buddy," the driver continued as they slowed in freeway traffic. "I know a place you could stay for the same price and it's like a friggin' palace, inna good neighborhood, too. Friend of mine owns it and only takes guests he likes. He'd take you, though, on my say-so."

Jackie was intrigued. "Why would you recommend me? You don't even know me."

The cabbie didn't say anything, busy now, moving from lane to lane and cursing other drivers.

A Transaction In Souls

"Well, I'm a good judge of character," he replied, stopped again. "And I say that you're a guy with character but with a problem, too. I'd like to help. And then maybe you can help me, too, sometime."

Here it comes, Jackie thought. But the driver didn't add anything except, "So would you maybe like a look? Can't hurt to look."

Against his better judgment but curious too, Jackie went along with it. He asked the name of the hotel and the cabbie said it didn't have one. And there was that laugh again, but this time friendlier.

The rest of the ride consisted of Jackie asking questions about the hotel and Crazy Tony answering his inquiries in a way that told him little. He did drop that it was "enchanted," then changed that to "enchanting." He mentioned that some famous people had stayed there but he couldn't remember names. Finally, they pulled in front of an attractive yet slightly foreboding black and gray Victorian on a quiet street lined with trees and front yards.

Crazy Tony was out of the cab and opening the door, smiling. "Come on and take a look. It don't hurt to look."

Oh alright, Jackie thought in a devil-may-care mood.

He got out and looked around. "Just go in," Crazy Tony called out, heading for the trunk. "It's always open." The cabbie opened the trunk and hoisted Jackie's suitcase onto his back like a sailor. The door was open, but it was dark inside and Jackie stood there, waiting for his eyes to adjust. He was startled the next moment when he felt something brush the back of his

A Loud Humming Sound Came From Above

neck. But there wasn't anything there. Now he heard voices from another room. Gradually, he could make out the space: the furnishings were from a couple of centuries past, which gave him the sensation of having traveled back in time. Pinpoints of light coming from somewhere in the back gave the room more definition.

Crazy Tony was standing there, expressionless. "Come on, Mister Grisman, let me show you a room."

They boarded a small black elevator that transported them to the floor above. It opened onto a hallway where the day's fading light was dappling the peeling rose wallpaper. Crazy Tony produced a skeleton key, stuck it into a door, and turned and opened it.

The room contained glossy, black furniture. The walls were wide horizontal stripes of dull red and charcoal. An antique floor lamp stood by an overstuffed chair. The bedspread was embroidered with a design and script that made Jackie think of ancient Egypt. On the black dresser was a sculpture that looked like an occult artifact: a silver disk supported by what appeared to be coiled snakes. The dresser mirror had an elaborate frame and a gray cast. He looked into it but didn't recognize himself at first. He found the bathroom: spotless, all glass and mirrors, a big sunken tub, and a smell of lavender in the air. Jackie began to feel a touch of elation, something that he hadn't experienced for a long time.

The phone rang with a soft purr and he spotted it on a low ebony table. It was an old, heavy black phone. He picked it up.

"Hello?"

A Transaction In Souls

A voice with an even softer purr asked: "Mr. Grisman, does the room meet your requirements?"

"It's very nice. How much?"

"Pay what you think it's worth when you decide to leave."

Jackie laughed. "Okay, how about twenty dollars a day?"

"That'll be fine," the voice on the line answered, then wished him a good night before the connection was cut. Jackie shrugged and placed the phone back in its cradle. He started to unpack, although he couldn't remember the cabbie having brought up his bag. He shrugged again but had another fleeting feeling that the place was haunted in some way, even though he didn't believe in that nonsense.

Jackie opened the window and looked down to a garden surrounded by red brick walls. Jungle plants wrapped around bamboo poles and hung from some crossbeams in a small sheltered area; mushroom shaped seats, straight from a fairy tale, were placed here and there; and a black trash can was set off to one side with a rake leaning against it. Not much of a jump, he thought, but he really didn't feel like snuffing it at the moment. The strange cabbie and now this odd hotel held him in a curious mood, and he hadn't been curious about anything for a long time.

While soaking in the tub, Jackie decided he would go downtown and eat at some tourist spot. After dressing, he took the elevator back down to the lobby. Jackie noticed someone sitting in one of the overstuffed chairs, smoking a pipe. The whiff he got was pleasing, and like nothing he had ever smelled

A Loud Humming Sound Came From Above

before. He couldn't make out the man's face in the dim lighting.

"What an interesting smell," Jackie said to the faceless man across the room.

He recognized the purring voice from the phone: "It's something I picked up in a little shop in Istanbul, and I've blended it with some forbidden tobacco given to me by a mad monk in Budapest."

Jackie laughed. "That's a good one," heading towards the front door.

"Where to, Mister Grisman?" the man asked.

Jackie stopped. "Oh, just downtown to get some dinner," wondering who this guy was.

"Well, dinner is almost ready here, sir. And it comes with the rental of the room."

"Is that so? Well then, count me in." Jackie strode over closer to the man in the chair and took his own seat. Jackie could finally see that the man was old—very old, yet keen and bright as a cat. There was something of the gnome about him and his eyes were even more penetrating than the cabbie's. The remaining hair on the sides of his head was cut very close. He was wearing a red ascot and a black velvet smoking jacket. He smiled thinly and puffed his pipe.

"Would you care for a cocktail before dinner?" he asked.

"Well, sure, whiskey and soda, please." Jackie was now feeling the comfort of the chair and the room.

"I'm Doctor Savoy, the owner and master of this residence," he explained, extending a cold hand.

"Well, Doc," Jackie said, "This sure is some deal. I don't quite get it though, I gotta tell you. And you

A Transaction In Souls

know, I didn't pay that cabbie...ah, Crazy Tony?"

"It's been taken care of. It'll be included on your final bill."

"Well, you think of everything."

A new presence entered the room: an elegant young lady carrying a silver tray with a drink on it. She wore her hair short, her skirt shorter, and a sexy black bra that brushed Jackie's face as she bent over to place his drink on a coaster. She looked briefly into his eyes, giving him a thrill, and there was that lavender scent again. She straightened up, turned, and sashayed off into another dimly lit room.

"Wow!" Jackie said to the doctor, but the old man was no longer there. He took a stiff pull on his drink.

As Jackie was sucking on an ice cube, the girl strolled back into the room to announce that dinner was served. He followed her into an ample, empty dining room and was shown to a seat at the end of a long table. The girl uncovered his platter and walked off. The roast lamb with mint, like his mother used to make, made his mouth water; the mashed potatoes, corn on the cob, and warm rolls were equally as satisfying. He didn't even mind that he was the only one eating. The place was screwy, he thought, but who cares? He tried a glass of the Beaujolais and found it to be superb.

Afterward, Jackie sat back and loosened his belt and looked around for a toothpick. On cue, the girl came back into the room with a piece of blueberry pie and a small pot of coffee. She placed a dollop of whipped cream on the pie and walked away again. After he polished off the pie, he stepped outside for

A Loud Humming Sound Came From Above

some air. He sat in the odd little garden he'd seen from his room and decided not to go out after all. He'd turn in early and get a good night's rest, then go out in the morning. Life was not looking so bad, he thought.

In his room, Jackie undressed, got into bed, and closed his eyes, but found he couldn't sleep. He kept thinking about the old mirror on the dresser. He sat up and looked over at it. Nothing unusual. He turned on a lamp. It's just a mirror after all, he thought. But then a white cat with blazing eyes was sitting on the dresser. It leapt into the mirror and disappeared. Jackie swallowed hard.

Now I'm seeing things, he thought. He got up and stood in front of the old mirror. He looked into it and was drawn into a scene that was gradually coming to life. I must be losing my mind, he thought, as two Minotaurs with arms crossed flanked a group of naked female dancers swaying from side to side. Some lay on the ground writhing, moaning. There were tall palms in the background and bejeweled elephants, and the sound of jangly rhythms, drums, and flutes. He could almost touch the dancers and feel the torrid climate. Then it was all gone. He kept looking into the mirror, blinking, but could only see his somewhat disheveled face.

"I must be delirious," Jackie thought as he climbed back into the bed. He closed his eyes, then bolted upright. The waitress, now naked, was straddling him and smiling devilishly. "I'm Alicia," she whispered and licked his ear. Jackie, who'd had no desire for sex in the past year, became aroused as she gyrated. He turned her over, and like a crazed satyr,

30

A Transaction In Souls

went to work. Afterward she murmured, "Maybe you can do something for me sometime?" That was what Crazy Tony had said, Jackie thought, seeing a shadow quickly climb the wall.

"And maybe you can do something for me?" piped up the old man's voice and Jackie saw him sitting there in the overstuffed chair. Alicia slithered out of bed and disappeared.

"Look back into the mirror," Doctor Savoy said in a dark, commanding voice. Jackie looked—the mirror appeared to be right before him. He could see scenes from his life unfolding, all filled with the disappointment and despair that formed the empty shell of his existence. More images from his past flickered by, making him wince and want to look away.

"You were going to kill yourself." Savoy spoke in a mocking tone. "I see why."

"Who are you?" Jackie asked, awestruck. The mirror was now back on the dresser.

"I'm the one offering you a better life, life as it's been for the last few hours," the old man replied with a chuckle. "And more."

"For what?"

"At the risk of sounding like an old cornball, your soul."

Alicia was now back in the room, moving suggestively at the foot of the bed. Jackie found a pipe in his hand with the wonderful-smelling tobacco smoldering in it. He took a puff and felt a warmth blossom in his heart and spread through his entire body. He remembered a short period when he had been a happy child. "It's a deal," he agreed, and everything

31

A Loud Humming Sound Came From Above

became a delicious, swirling vortex...

Crazy Tony was carrying a suitcase on his back and speaking to a tall, bookish man who was looking around the front yard of the hotel with an intrigued expression. He didn't seem to notice Jackie. "Come on and have a look," Crazy Tony was saying. "It don't hurt to look. Go ahead in. It's always open."

Jackie continued to rake up the leaves. Next, he would trim the bushes, and then do whatever else the Master wanted, including feeding the foul, moaning things in the basement. He would do anything to not become like them.

As You Wish

Taylor Reed sat in a café looking at a fountain across the street. Behind the fountain stood a dilapidated, derelict, and yet, at one time, elegant hotel. Matisse was reported to have stayed and worked there during one of his sojourns. "One day," Taylor thought, "I'll give the watchman ten dirham for a look inside."

Taylor ruminated over his last three years of living in Morocco. He spent the first year mostly drinking endless coffees and mint teas in the cafés. And smoking hashish and kif—a tobacco and marijuana mixture—in cafés of a different sort. He would drift back and forth between the expat crowd of writers, painters, musicians, and assorted eccentrics, and his Moroccan friends. Sometimes, the two crowds converged, but they usually remained separate. During the first year, he hadn't been certain whether he had any real talent as a painter. His work proved exciting but was sporadic. Now he could look back on most of the pieces he had done then with more affection than disdain. He remembered being happy just looking out his window at the garden across from him, and over the rooftops at the cobalt blue Strait of Gibraltar that filled him with ideas of mythology and adventure.

The second year, he traveled: Agadir, Marrakech,

A Loud Humming Sound Came From Above

Essaouira, Fez, Meknes, and, closer to home, he spent time in Asilah, Ksar es-Seghir, and the little blue town in the Rif Mountains, Chefchaouen. He had covered countless canvasses, and felt himself coming into his own. Color broke free for him. And the colors of Morocco were like no others: The reds were redder, the yellows were a yellow you could taste, and they all filled his palette. The light of Morocco seemed from another world entirely. He had painted the veiled women, the date palms at the edge of the Sahara, the valleys of wildflowers, the heady, medieval souks. The intricacies of the carpet designs and tapestries had spun his mind into a pleasant delirium as he worked away in kif-induced trances.

During the third year, he felt he had discovered the city of Tangier in a way that was not open to everyone—especially not to a foreigner. He also discovered magic, witnessed it, experienced it. He decided then that this was where he'd stay.

Lately, he was just enjoying the simple life, the easy pace. Even with Morocco moving gradually, steadfastly into the modern world, it remained ancient, and this pleased him and others of a like mind. Of course, the days of Paul Bowles—hell, even the days of Rolling Stone Brian Jones savoring Jajouka music—were long gone, but still, something of those times stubbornly remained. Something else too: something older and indefinable would always be there, no matter what. Staring at the mosaic floor in the café and the curlicues of design over the arched doorway, he experienced again that ecstatic feeling of being outside of time in this whitewashed city, on hills

As You Wish

that overlooked a bay that could have been filled with blue ink.

Taylor realized that someone was observing him. The observer, a young Westerner, seemed put out when Taylor caught his eye, as though he had just been caught stealing, and, once spotted, dashed off. Taylor decided to pursue him. He followed him across the Grand Socco in the hot midday sun, knowing he'd lose him in the Medina. But Taylor knew he'd see him again, too. Tangier was like that. When he did, he'd strike up a conversation with him and see what his story was.

That very evening, he saw him again. The boy was at Club Zewa, sitting with some other young tourists and they all looked a little drunk. He spied Taylor and smiled with what Taylor considered an insolent expression. Taylor went to the bar and ordered a cold Heineken "from the back of the fridge." A Moroccan he knew was sitting there eating peanuts and drinking a tall glass of whiskey. He, too, was inebriated but cheerfully greeted Taylor with good will and a toast that Taylor couldn't comprehend. Taylor smiled and tipped his beer at him. Taylor looked at the reflection of the group in a large brass vase behind the bar and saw that the boy was gone. He turned around and scanned the room. The boy was nowhere in sight. Taylor moved off with his beer and went outside into the garden area. The boy was sitting alone at a table, with his own Heineken, grinning. He gestured for Taylor to join him and he did.

"My name is Kyle Davis and I wish to tell you a story," he began. Taylor smiled and said okay.

A Loud Humming Sound Came From Above

"Last year, while on a short visit here, I was walking along Boulevard Pasteur early one evening. A beautiful sunset was just dying and I stopped for a minute to observe the palms and the bay below. Suddenly, I was accosted and knocked to the ground by a young Moroccan. The strap to my shoulder bag broke and he kicked me as I lay on the ground stunned. He took my bag, which contained my camera, keys, floppy disks, and other small items, then ran off quickly.

"I had never been mugged or robbed before. 'Voleur! Voleur!' I yelled at several passing petit taxi drivers and the men working on a building nearby. In less than a minute, a butagas cart came speeding past to chase the mugger. Two or three minutes later, the robber was caught, and the butagas cart driver came back to retrieve me. He took me to the Merkala police station where a line of Sécuritié Nationale vans were parked in front. Inside, I saw the thief in a corner in handcuffs. A policeman asked me to identify him. I did, and then I got all my belongings back. I spent an hour at the station answering questions and the policeman in charge occasionally would step into another room to hit the thief with a stick. With my mobile phone, which was also in the bag, I called my friends and told them what had happened. Finally, I was driven back to the hotel but the next morning, I was so sore, I stayed in bed all day resting. Why am I telling you this story?"

Taylor shrugged.

"Since this same man now works for you, I'm worried about your safety. I know your work, Mr. Reed. I also want to paint, and regardless of that unfortunate experience, I've decided to live here, too, at least part of the year. I have a small business in New York I must attend to a few months of the year."

"He works for me?" Taylor asked. "Nobody except Fatima, my maid, works for me. I believe you're mistaken."

"But I saw him on various occasions delivering material to your house, and to a café a few times."

"You're talking about Drissi," Taylor said, wondering why this boy had him under surveillance. Conveniently, Drissi was away for the summer. But Taylor played it off and laughed. "Well, come to think of it, Drissi was once a thief, but that was when he was very young. In fact, he spent a time in jail. But he's long reformed and has since become a poet. I think you've confused him with someone else."

The boy didn't look convinced.

"But Kyle," Taylor asked, "why have you been watching me so closely?"

Kyle looked uncomfortable for only a second. Then he said quickly, "I'm one of your creations. I've escaped from one of your paintings."

Taylor was laughing now and thinking the boy was an interesting character even for Tangier. Taylor studied his impish eyes and bread-white complexion, the tight mouth that revealed little. Taylor lit a cigarette.

"Is that so? Which one, pray tell?"

Kyle allowed a slight smile. "Well, it's untitled but was used for the cover of Jesse Higgins's *Danger USA*."

The piece that Kyle referred to was taken from

a dream and had always made Taylor a little uneasy though he didn't know why. It was based on a rough sketch he had made after waking suddenly from a dream. All he had been able to recall was two hands in a frame. That constituted the sketch and the minimal painting that followed. One hand was clenched in a fist and the other was emulating a gun. Jesse had wanted it right away for his short story collection and, although Taylor was reluctant, he went ahead and let him use it.

Taylor forced a laugh. "But that was only hands."

"Yes, but they're my hands." Kyle imitated the piece with his hands in the air, giving Taylor an eerie feeling.

"You dreamt them right?" Kyle asked.

"I did," Taylor said.

Kyle continued, "I had a similar dream. In my dream, they were my hands and I made a rough sketch when I awoke. Then I saw the Higgins book and I began researching you. I made my first trip here, although it was cut short by the mugging and the illness of two people in the party I was traveling with. But now I'm back and on my own."

"Well, I've got to say that's interesting and original. You wouldn't happen to have that sketch with you?"

"Of course, Mister Reed," Kyle pulled a bound notebook out of his backpack. The book was filled with strange drawings, cutouts from magazines and newspapers, and notes or diary entries. Kyle located the drawing and handed it over. It could have been the same initial sketch Taylor had made a couple of years

As You Wish

ago. No one had ever seen that sketch. A slight prickly feeling went up Taylor's back and circled his head, and he felt dizzy for a moment. He thought maybe his drink had been spiked but then the feeling passed. He looked at this young man whose expression revealed nothing.

"So what can I do for you?" Taylor asked evenly.

The boy smiled ever so slightly. "I would like to pose for you, Mister Reed. I would like to commission you to paint my portrait. I'll pay the price you ask."

Taylor lit another cigarette. He hadn't done any work lately and was even thinking of traveling again to get the juices going. But here was a unique opportunity: a strange proposition from a peculiar character. And why not? He could paint him in the garden and work only the days Fatima was there, since there was an oddly uncomfortable element to the whole deal. The young man may very well be mad, but that wasn't exactly new territory for Taylor. He felt challenged and curious about painting the mysterious young man's portrait. Taylor named a fair price and stated which days and hours he would work on it, and Kyle readily agreed. They closed the deal with another drink and talked a little shop. Taylor was impressed that Kyle knew his subject and sounded a lot like Taylor himself when he had first dreamed of becoming a painter. Kyle wrote out a Bank of America check with a New York address. Taylor would take it to the bank the next day, and wait to see if it indeed was good. He set their first date for a week later to make sure.

The day arrived for their first session. It was a pleasant day and the garden was arranged with

A Loud Humming Sound Came From Above

umbrellas and a refreshment table with tea, Sidi Harazem water bottles in a bucket of ice, fruit, and croissants. Caesar, Taylor's old tomcat, sat in the chair designated for the subject and surveyed his domain skeptically. Taylor had decided that he would not show Kyle the daily progress but rather cover it at the end of each session and show him only the final work. As he was double-checking his implements, he overheard voices and looked up to see a smirking Kyle Davis wearing a striped djellaba and a red fez with tassel cocked to the side of his head. Fatima, standing behind him, gave Taylor a troubled look, then disappeared back into the kitchen.

"Oh, Mister Reed, I still can't believe it. A dream come true," Kyle said, extending his hand.

Taylor shook it and said, "Well, you look very 'Maroc.' Folkloric."

"Yes, isn't it splendid? It's as close as I'll get to Lawrence of Arabia."

"All you need is a horse and a rusty rifle," Taylor said and moved Caesar to another seat. The old cat begrudgingly accepted the unexpected transport.

"Kyle, I'd like you to call me Taylor." He gestured to the refreshments and Kyle smiled, took his assigned seat, and produced a sebsi, or kif pipe, in two parts from his big pocket. He attached them and expertly nuzzled a small clay bowl onto the end. He filled the bowl from a pouch and offered it. Taylor, however, had already produced his own pipe and said, "Go ahead. Is that with or without spice?" He noticed Kyle's pipe was identical to his own.

"No tobacco, but a touch of hashish," Kyle

As You Wish

acknowledged with a wink. Taylor accepted the leather pouch, which was also like his own. It was especially good kif. And he could smell the pungent hashish. Taylor wondered how the boy had gotten hooked up so quickly but decided not to pry. They sat and puffed on their sebsis; Fatima appeared through a cloud of smoke, delivering short glasses of piping hot mint tea, essential for the kif smoker's throat.

After tea, the work began. The previous day, Taylor had spread linseed oil over the first layer of eggshell white. He began now with pencil and then switched to paint. The red ochre perfectly matched the wide stripe of the djellaba.

Over the next several weeks, the sessions passed and Kyle was a perfect subject, keeping the pose that Taylor preferred and speaking only when questioned. The only other sounds were occasional Arabic music from a neighbor's radio, the chirping of birds, and the distant horn blast of a ferry arriving from Spain. When they heard the afternoon prayer call, it was their cue to stop for the day. Kyle had no problem with not seeing the work and didn't peek or complain.

As for the portrait, it was coming along, but Taylor was having trouble with the eyes, which as the hours passed began to resemble those of a lizard or wild bird. Then, suddenly, they would resume their odd, sedate yet impish, stare. Sometimes they would glow or reflect light in an odd way. Other times, the iris looked as though it was opening like some exotic flower right in front of him. Kyle seemed to sense Taylor's difficulty and would look away, forcing Taylor to scold him. There were moments when the face in

43

A Loud Humming Sound Came From Above

the painting would go black, and the faces of other people Taylor knew would flash before him.

Taylor wiped a bead of sweat off his brow. He tried to concentrate but the tone, the color, the light and dark would change course from minute to minute.

One day, Taylor asked if he could take a few photographs and, for the first time, Kyle was visibly upset.

"No photographs please. I have a real aversion to having my picture taken. I realize it would help you but I must insist."

"As you wish," Taylor said, repeating the common Moroccan expression.

He studied his work and was pleased except for the eyes. He had not captured them yet and he now tried to photograph them with his mind. Kyle seemed to sense this as he said his good-byes for the day.

Once alone, Taylor quickly did some sketches. One he particularly liked almost caught the odd juxtaposition of mischievousness and calmness that the boy's eyes possessed. He went to his canvas and tacked up the drawing. He smoked a bowl of kif and looked until he was seeing both the drawing and the canvas at the same time. He fell into a trance and began to work.

Taylor awoke on the bench, covered with Moroccan blankets, on his cushions made by a tribe in the high Alas Mountains. It was twilight and he felt invigorated as he sat up and looked over at the portrait. He walked toward it as moonlight spilled into his small garden. The portrait of Kyle Davis was finished and the eyes were something to behold. They persistently

As You Wish

drew the viewer toward them and into their sphere, triggering a feeling of recognition that could not be explained. Taylor got lost in them, standing there in the moonlight, and wondered what the real story was with the mysterious young man. He delicately printed his initials and the date in the lower right corner. He would give Kyle his portrait the following day.

But the time came for Kyle to arrive and he did not appear. After an hour, Taylor took the painting inside. He realized he didn't even know where the young man was staying. And he didn't know anyone else who knew him, which was strange in Tangier. He would just have to wait until he heard from him.

After a few days had passed, Taylor began to ask around but no one else seemed to have ever noticed the lad at all. Taylor began to wonder if the boy was a djinn—some genie or ghost. Taylor had had profound life-changing experiences with djinns and the magic of Morocco the previous year, although others might consider it a psychopathology at best.

He decided to visit an old friend named Omar who had come back to Tangier from Fez for the summer. They sat in Omar's sister's front room, sipping tea and smoking kif, and Taylor told him the story. As Omar poured more tea from his old, darkened samovar, he said, "If he does not come back he is a djinn. If he returns, he was possessed."

Three years earlier, Taylor would've thought this a quaint idea, but now, after his own experiences in this realm, he believed Omar.

Weeks passed and Taylor moved on to other things. He worked on a series of pieces using drawings

A Loud Humming Sound Came From Above

of Caesar's eyes and some abstract experiments that, together, took on the appearance of alien, mythological landscapes. As he was putting the finishing touches to one of these, he heard his bell. Fatima was off, so he went down to see who it was. A small Moroccan beggar boy stood on his step, holding a large blue envelope. He handed it to Taylor who used some friendly Arabic to stop him from running off. The boy smiled but continued to stare at the ground. Taylor opened the envelope and extracted a neatly-typed missive that he noticed right away was signed by Kyle Davis.

> *Dear Taylor,*
> *Please forgive my disappearance, but there was no other way. Come to the Rembrandt Hotel immediately and I'll explain everything. I look forward to seeing you and finally having my portrait, which I know must be done.*
>
> *Sincerely,*
> *Kyle Davis*

Taylor gave the boy a couple of dirham and watched him run off. He took a shower, dressed, and sat smoking a cigarette, examining the portrait before he would wrap it and deliver it. It was definitely finished and it was a smashing piece of work. He felt almost like he had not painted it at all; he wondered if perhaps a djinn had entered his mind and guided his hand during that entire period.

Taylor leaned closer to the portrait, getting a

whiff of something alien and foul. Lightning seemed to flash in his head and he stared at the painting for a long while. A chill had come over him, and a gloom seemed to drift all around him. Finally, Caesar came into the room, breaking the trance. Taylor looked at the clock on the wall and saw that it was time to wrap the painting and leave.

On the walk to the hotel, Taylor fought off a nagging sense that he'd forgotten something. He felt a sourness in his stomach and wondered if he was going to be sick. He sat at an outdoor café and waved the waiter away. He wiped the sweat from his brow. The waiter delivered a glass of water anyway and Taylor drank it. Slowly, he began to feel better. He left the café and continued on his way, the portrait now heavy in his hands.

At the Rembrandt Hotel, the front desk clerk told him which room Monsieur Davis was in. Taylor saw waves of colors pour through the foyer and a lightning flash in his head knocked him against the desk. The clerk and Taylor glanced at each other knowing something unexplainable, unknowable had just occurred. The clerk looked for his prayer beads and Taylor picked up his painting and headed up the stairway.

Kyle's room was at the end of a hallway. As Taylor approached, he saw that the door was slightly ajar. The room looked to be swirling in lights like a damned discothèque and Taylor edged the door open with his toe.

Before him, Kyle was levitating as colors splattered the room and escaped in every direction.

47

A Loud Humming Sound Came From Above

There was a high-pitched yowl and Taylor saw in a mirror behind Kyle a creature covered in a clear slime. It looked like a hideous hybrid of a human and an eel, its eyes demon red. The djinn's hands mimicked the original sketch that Kyle claimed to be his own. Taylor turned away, tore the wrapping off the portrait and positioned it toward the mirror. At first, the djinn only gloated, but when Kyle gasped and fell to the floor, it shrieked and then screamed.

Taylor turned and faced it with the portrait. He approached the djinn despite the shrieking and hissing. Finally, it leapt toward the open window, leaving behind the same foul smell Taylor had detected before he'd wrapped the painting.

Kyle, mostly recovered, gazed at his portrait and said, "I—I can never thank you enough, Taylor. I knew only you could possibly get me out of this. After all, you drew my hands. But I couldn't tell you anything about what was happening."

Kyle took the cigarette that Taylor offered. They smoked silently and listened to the traffic noises from the busy Boulevard Pasteur below them.

"Welcome to Tangier," Taylor finally said.

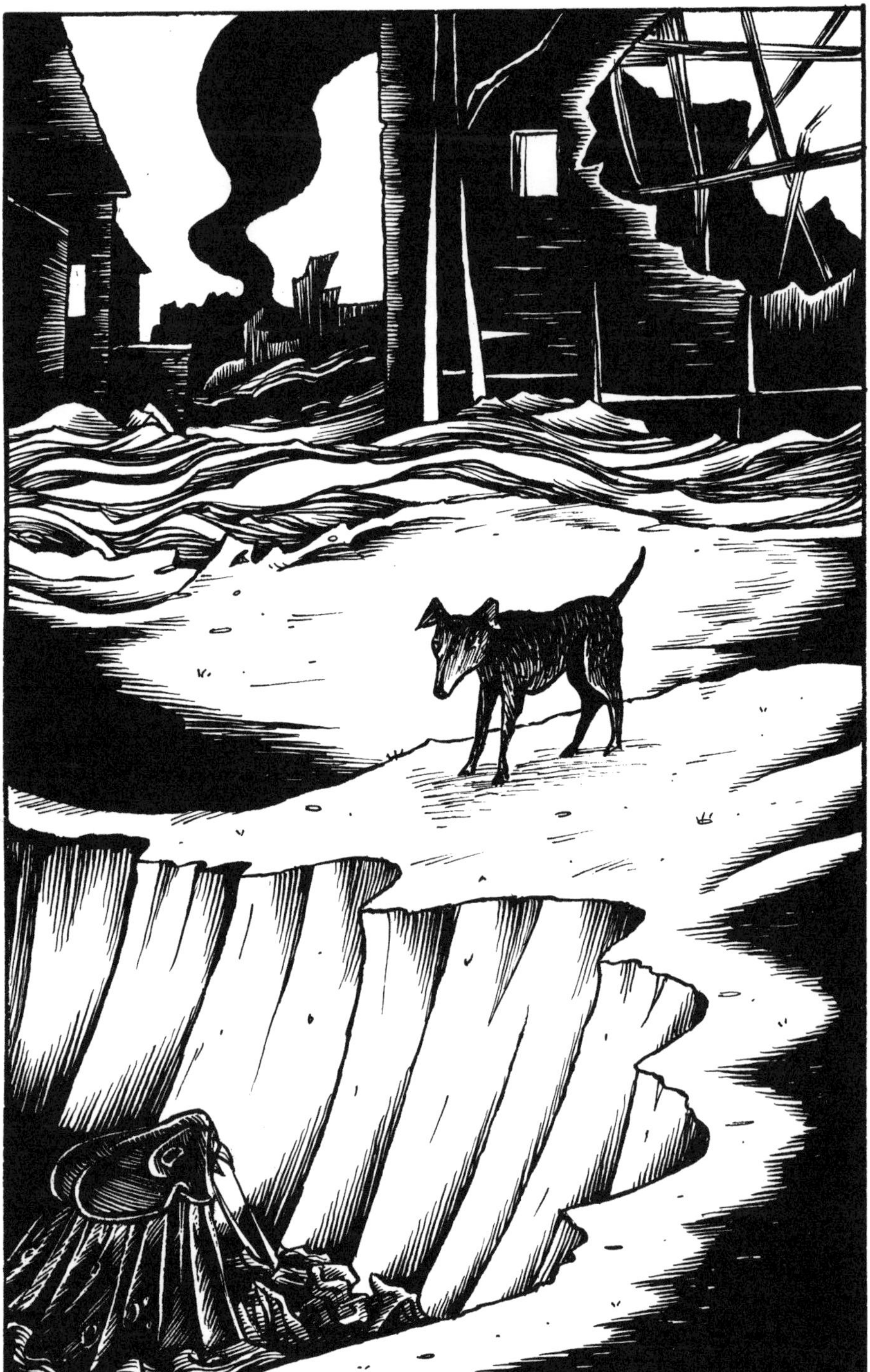

Night Flamers

A dazed, short, fat man with a buzz cut stood in the street, waving a handgun. He turned and fired a shot into the empty doorway of an apartment complex. The gunman then crossed the street and disappeared into the doorway.

A white 1956 Oldsmobile rolled along California Street, using the last of its gas. The cars it passed in the street were all empty. A tour bus and an ersatz cable car, empty as well, stood near the entrance of the Mark Hopkins Hotel. The front tires of the Oldsmobile just made it onto the red brick forecourt of the hotel as the car died.

Two people got out. The driver, Dr. Rodriguez from Buenos Aires, had originally come to California to attend a convention on life extension and present his paper on the results of a study of 17 spider monkeys treated with a synthesis of longevity drugs. The passenger, Rita, a striking Korean beauty and a professional escort and masseuse, had been with the doctor at his hotel at the time of The Invasion. They were among the few thousand who had escaped from Los Angeles. At a hundred miles per hour, they had raced past blackened ruins; the horrible images still remained in their unsettled minds.

A Loud Humming Sound Came From Above

In San Francisco, they had seen only one other person: a snarling woman dressed and made up as a clown. Rita had gestured wildly and yelled to her, but the angry clown had run off and disappeared behind a mound of burning debris.

With furrowed brows, Dr. Rodriguez watched Rita walk through the revolving glass door into the lobby of the Mark. Upstairs, they found an open suite and Rita collapsed onto the bed. The doctor looked at the back of her bare thighs and for a moment wanted to caress her. His mind was still racing. He looked at the phone on the nightstand; he knew it was dead. He sat on a beige velvet couch and tried the TV remote. Dead, of course. Unable to sleep, Rita moaned, got up, and looked through the closets, where she found pieces of a woman's wardrobe. In the bathroom, she had a sponge bath, using the water she found in a pitcher. She tried on an elegant silver evening gown. Expressionless, she looked at herself in the full-length mirror. She lit a cigarette. She wondered if she was losing her mind.

Night fell, and an all-encompassing blackness blotted out the city. Dr. Rodriguez and Rita sat by the window, looking out at the sky. They watched a dirigible passing above the Transamerica Building like an enormous, slow, gray bullet. A detachment of soldiers parachuted down to the streets. Lights were attached to their helmets. Their eyes were partially hidden behind tinted wraparounds. Rita felt as if she was watching a deranged, speeded-up film as the soldiers began their methodical search.

In a back yard behind a modest house was a

Night Flamers

small, black terrier named TJ. The dog was looking wildly at a deep crater. A minute earlier, he had witnessed something emerge from it that had stilled his usually persistent bark. The head had resembled the skull of some extinct denizen of the deep. A pulsing green membrane had run down from its thick neck, circling its dully-gleaming torso. The thing had emitted an ear-splitting screech that had drowned out TJ's growl, then it had burst into the sky. The dog ran yelping back into the house. The occupants, his owners, had vanished two days prior. The dog whimpered, lay back down, and continued to wait.

The next morning, TJ, following his instinct, ran off down the empty streets. He stopped at an old house where the garage door was open. The dog smelled food cooking somewhere nearby. Cautiously, he looked in. There stood a little girl who squealed with delight at seeing him, but he ran off in fright. TJ was seeking someone more like his previous masters. He stayed hidden while the girl called out, "Here, doggy. Here, doggy."

A while later, the little girl and two other diminutive people came out of the garage and shut the door behind them. Like the little girl, they, too, were deeply tanned, wore blonde wigs and had white lips. All three wore small backpacks and each carried a little rifle. With anxious brown eyes, TJ watched them walk down the snow-covered street and disappear around a corner.

TJ made his way around to the back of the house and sniffed at the air. He saw two old men sitting on a porch swing, wearing party hats, embracing. The

A Loud Humming Sound Came From Above

men saw the dog, disengaged, and began inviting him, coaxing him, to approach. TJ wagged his tail and gradually went up onto the porch. One man went inside and came back with a dish of unfamiliar food and a bowl of water. TJ lapped greedily at the water with his small red tongue. As the dog drank, he became aware of an enormous shadow approaching. A loud humming sound came from above and one of the men snatched him up protectively and they all rushed inside.

Freak weather conditions came next. A relentless hot wind from some infernal place was followed by a dusting of pale, yellow snow. The sky was filled with static and, to some of the remaining survivors, the dark clouds began to form faces.

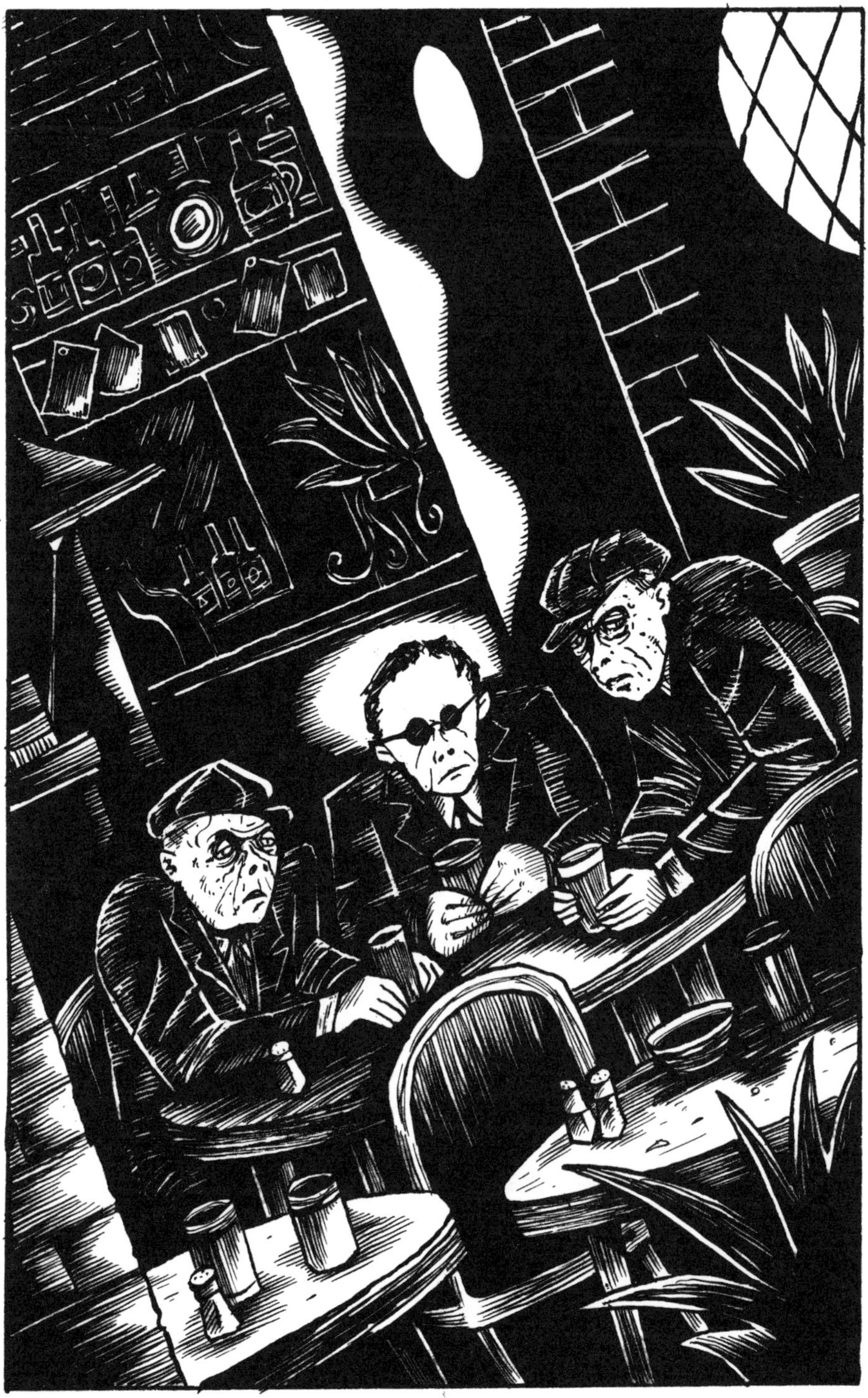

OTHER PORTS, OTHER HELLS

On the island, Jamie rode his bike past the once grand, now crumbling, mansions, their pillar-fronted verandahs arranged with dilapidated furniture and overgrown with leafy plants. Pine, coconut palms, mangrove, and sea grape flourished throughout the island. The yellow leaves of the plane trees littered the windy roads. In the village, he passed tourists, guides, money exchange booths, information givers, and gewgaw stands. He pedaled on and stopped near the docks. A lurching gull landed on a pylon—part of a skeletal dock that gradually disappeared into the oily, green sea. Jamie stared at the point where the ocean and the sky seemed to meet and create a golden shimmer. Behind him, the village glowed, looking like a film set for a fairy tale. He rolled off toward the loading docks and found Elias surrounded by their gear, wearing a slightly tattered khaki outfit and smoking a fragrant cigar.

"Once, in Malaysia, I had dealings with an errant tribe who tattooed their backs with the five-pointed star," Elias said, after Jamie sat down on a piece of luggage. "Their shaman, after a psychedelic trip, drew me a picture of the assassin who was on my trail. To elude him, I traveled by boat, car, and train for weeks,

A Loud Humming Sound Came From Above

crisscrossing most of Southeast Asia, playing the part of a Brit, drinking gin and tonics—all those slices of lime sinking into melting ice—and using phrases like 'dog and bone' and calling my flashlight a 'torch.'

"At a way station, I finally took him out: a Greek hit man who went by the absurd name of Spooky. He was having a cigarette. With a quick thrust of my kajar, I stopped him in the middle of an exhale, then pulled out the blade slowly." Elias's eyes glowed dimly at the recollection. "As I made my escape on a river barge, I remember the temple rooftops visible in the distance against a blue evening sky."

The restaurant Elias had chosen was expensive. A woman with a shrieking, ugly, little boy entered the room. Elias made eye contact with the brat, who fell silent, as though stricken mute. The woman, just short of amazement, nodded a thank-you but Elias remained stone-faced. Muted cumbia instrumentals played on a hidden sound system. A wacked-out wah-wah guitar accompanied a Latin dance beat. Elias fished out a business card from his sleeve, glanced at it, then put it away.

At the back of the restaurant were a couple of pool tables in front of tall, shuttered windows. Two players, both with heavy-lidded eyes and wearing small caps jauntily to the side, chewed on toothpicks. Out a closer window, a pathway of worn bricks imbedded in the sand led to the beach. Across the way, yellow, blue, orange, red, and green washing hung on lines. The sky turned dark and raindrops as big as coins began to splatter the panes.

"Last night, the natives dressed up like monkeys," Elias said, poking at a piece of rubbery display fruit on the table. "It was marvelous. Did you hear the drumming?"

"I did, but I couldn't rouse myself," Jamie answered, looking a little spaced-out.

"Well, you missed quite a show. But there should be more tomorrow night."

The soup was delivered by a thin, dark waiter wearing a gaudy striped shirt. Jamie looked into the soup bowl and then closed his eyes: the whole universe seemed to be exploding inside his head: a line of Roman Candles went off, shooting stars and white strobe flashes behind his eyes. He opened his eyes, cleared his head, and looked out the window at a blazing sun that had appeared after the squall.

"Our waiter here was born in Lima," Elias said, "but is trying to learn English and save enough money to make his way to the States and become an American. He has a cousin who owns a shoe repair business in Detroit." Elias shrugged with an expression of resignation. "Of course, you can't tell him he's making a colossal mistake. He'd think you were trying to trick him."

Across the room, a peculiar new customer had taken a table. The corners of his mouth pointed downward. He had a chalky complexion, as though wearing ghoulish stage makeup, and his hair was rust-colored and choppily cut. His eyes were hidden behind small, round, dark glasses. The pool players with the funny hats put up their cues and joined him. Jamie realized now that these were all Committeemen. The one with the white skin was a commander and the other two

A Loud Humming Sound Came From Above

agent drones or AD men.

Jamie thought back to earlier in the day when they had hiked past tombs, temples, and other elaborate structures that had befuddled him. When he'd pointed out certain ones to Elias, he'd answered with his own question: "Who were these ancient islanders who built these ceremonial complexes?" Jamie was certain that Elias knew quite well and would tell him once they'd completed their study of the island.

They'd passed more ruins, a huge swimming pool, and the Crocodile Spirit Temple. They'd walked across a stone bridge that traversed a lagoon—green as a cat's eyes. On the other side, they'd studied the totems of birdmen. And they both heard something uttered that sounded like "Googalog." They searched the nearby caves but saw no one.

"The spirits speak," Elias had announced.

At the restaurant, the trio across from them was ordering now—with some difficulty, it seemed, since it was taking them a lengthy amount of time. Afterward, they remained silent, apparently communicating telepathically.

The food arrived: a thick yet delicate white fish, sweet yams, and wild rice. On the side was a small plate of salad with slices of pineapple. Jamie glanced at the table of the three, who were quietly spooning their soup.

Once again, Jamie had a vision of the bridge, with dark leaves floating along the slow-moving lagoon, the peep-peep of the birds, and the distant sound of waves breaking on a beach.

They took their coffee out on the verandah. Jamie

Other Ports, Other Hells

looked over his cup at Elias: his skin resembled silk. The air appeared to fill with a silvery dust. Jamie was used to these effects but now, in this light, noticed the wear and tear on Elias's beige summer suit. Elias motioned toward the street where what looked like liquid streetcars were streaming by; the passengers' faces were owlish and identical.

"We can see that but others cannot," Elias said, sniffing a cigar.

Jamie watched a few more "Committee transports" before the vision vanished. In the street, a tall, withered man batted at the disturbed air and a squat, redheaded woman shrieked at an ambivalent sky. Across the way, an illuminated skull watched from a shop window.

"The passengers are headed for Guam," Elias explained. "I've notified Dan Roscoe, who's been drifting around those parts."

Sobbing peasant women passed by, holding their shawls tight. Grief-stricken men stood in doorways, their lips moving but no sound being uttered. "There's been a funeral," Elias said, and finally lit his cigar. "An old man who was much loved by the villagers."

Elias leaned back in his chair and spoke in a soft voice as mosquito coils burned between them. "A circle is a sphere of influence." He drew a circle in the air with his match. "The shadow is included in the ritual, usually within the circle. A mirror will raise spirits and can be used for travel. The dream that embodies the circle, the shadow, and the mirror is the path we seek." His expression appeared precognitive, bemused.

A Loud Humming Sound Came From Above

"The professional dreamers of Egypt slept on graves to better communicate with the dead," he said. "Tonight, we'll sleep in the caves we saw earlier. But first, I'll deal with the commander and you'll eliminate the others." A disquieting vision of violence passed through Jamie's mind. With some apprehension, he considered the bright, black, animal eyes of the agents, hidden behind their heavy lids. Elias seemed distant, preoccupied. Yet, when he looked back at Jamie, he was grinning.

"Just follow what I've taught you," he offered, knowing Jamie was feeling out of sorts, getting over a nasty bug. Besides, it'd been a long time since they'd had any run-ins with the Committee. Previous battles flashed through Jamie's mind and he felt a burst of familiar excitement.

Later, they left their huts and set off in opposite directions, agreeing to meet afterward near the caves. Jamie hurried along a path, through a field of tall weeds. He was armed with six throwing knives. To his right, a flock of silver birds took flight. He ran by an area of white cliffs, forty or fifty feet high where monkeys climbed across the rocks, as though trying to convey some strange message. Jamie climbed down to the meandering beach. He ran for a while, then headed to a higher, rocky area.

Once he'd climbed a bit, he spotted a cove on the other side, and a man sitting in the sand, his back against a wooden crate. The man stood and turned, having heard Jamie, but he was slow to react. He was deeply tanned, scraggly-haired, bearded, and barechested. His pants were short and frayed. A marooned castaway? He appeared a little drunk, maybe a little mad as well.

"Googalog," the man yelled, when Jamie showed himself.

"Hullo?" Jamie answered.

The man saluted in an exaggerated way and pointed out to sea.

"They're intergalactic in origin," the man shouted, "No doubt about it."

"Who is Googalog?" Jamie asked.

"Him," the castaway pointed again, but Jamie couldn't see anything on the horizon but a faint shimmer. The man was shimmering too, and transforming himself. The heavy lids. The funny hat. He was one of the agent drones. Armed now with a pronged spear, he moved quickly toward Jamie, who whipped one of his seven-inch BlackJet knives through the air. It found the AD man's neck with a horrible twang and the drone cried out, dropping his weapon, desperately grasping at the knife. As he fell to his knees, another BlackJet pierced his heart. On his side now, coughing blood, the drone slid back down to the beach and, after a quick, violent spasm, died. Jamie was ready with another knife, sensing the space around him, but the other AD man was apparently not in the area. Jamie watched the waves wash over the dead drone for a few moments before moving on.

High from the encounter, he ran along the beach, glad to have his old sense of skill and confidence back. He headed toward the small fishing village.

Jamie asked around and located the place where the drones were staying. He found the bungalow and

A Loud Humming Sound Came From Above

broke in. He pulled back a curtain to let in the fading light. He picked up a pack of cards and bent them back, sending them flying into the air. They scattered like leaves, drifting to the floor. He pulled apart the neatly made bed, tossing the blankets and sheets, then adding the contents of the drawers to the mess.

The second drone entered casually, stepped behind a dressing partition, and laughed shrilly. Clutching a knife, Jamie kicked the panel away, revealing an open window. Jamie climbed out and followed the drone down a dusky trail, with darkness rapidly approaching.

At the end of the path, the AD man emerged from behind a temple at one end of an empty park. He was approaching methodically with a sullen, contemptuous expression, holding a pronged spear identical to that used by the first drone. His face was pulsating and sweating and, to Jamie, the spear appeared to be growing longer with each step. He feinted to the side, pivoted, and threw it expertly. Jamie ducked and felt it whiz past his head. Now it was Jamie who pivoted and tossed a knife, but from that distance the drone easily dodged it.

Jamie pursued him through three massive archways in light so bright, it was painful. Time seemed to be slowing down dramatically. The AD man had disappeared again.

Jamie stood in a ruinous park, sensing him. The AD man stepped out from behind a trapezoid monument. A strap-on dildo dangled from his forehead like an obscene dowser. Jamie saw metal flash in both his hands: throwing stars. They both threw at the same

Other Ports, Other Hells

time, but a whirl of red dust blinded them. When it cleared, Jamie saw that his knife had missed, but the AD man was frantically rubbing his eyes and yelling curses. Jamie absorbed the moment, then threw one more, straight into his target's gut. The AD man grimaced, made a sound like a sick dog, and spit blood in all directions. Then he fell face forward into the red dirt. Behind him, in the distance, was a city cast in a soft blue light. Jamie dusted himself off and made his way back through the three archways, heading to the bridge that led to the tombs, the birdman structures, the caves, and Elias.

The mound where Elias stood was lit by moonbeams. Surrounded by a circle drawn in the dirt stood a new totem. Elias was smoking a cigar and admiring his handiwork. Jamie looked closely and saw that the face, flattened and blank, was that of the commander. The rest of his body was also attached to the tall, wooden totem.

Elias nodded. "Meet Commander Googalog."

Two months later, Jamie and a native boy came ashore on an undisclosed island somewhere in the South Pacific. From their small dinghy, they carried what supplies they could manage: canned goods, rice, salt, and bars of chocolate. Jamie and the boy trekked through the jungle for an hour, eventually hearing the sound of waterfalls. They came to a clearing and the ruins stood before them.

Jamie spotted Elias, wearing a sun hat and writing in a small notebook, at the foot of one of the statues. He called out and Elias looked in his direction

65

A Loud Humming Sound Came From Above

and waved. The boy had gone ahead to deliver the supplies to the camp while the other workers were having their lunch. Jamie joined Elias in the shade, under a partially ruined dome where he had set up folding chairs on the half dirt, half tile floor. They drank from their canteens.

"Were you able to get any tobaccy?"

"Just this." Jamie handed him the odd-shaped cheroots.

Elias frowned. "Actually these aren't half bad. I haven't seen them for...well, a long time. How was the trip?"

"Uneventful. The main island doesn't offer much and is crowded with NGO reps and explorer types."

"Nobody followed you?" Elias asked.

"No. And from the talk I overheard in the bars, everybody is heading for the northern archipelago. It's funny that people don't know these ruins are only three hours south."

"Well, they think this area has all been explored. And it has, but the earth sometimes swallows things whole and presents them again thousands, even millions, of years later. The people who built these strange ceremonial pyramids, obelisk dwellings, and fearsome statues defy all known data on island races."

Elias stood. "Come, you'll want to see the latest."

They crossed the clearing and descended the wide, vaulted stone stairway. High above the arched portal was a wider arched ceiling.

They approached two stern guards at the entrance who muttered a greeting. They entered a deep room.

Other Ports, Other Hells

Elias adjusted a mobile generator and lights began coming on here and there. The room was filled with treasures: alabaster vases as big as a man, reliefs of strange creatures—perhaps the gods of these people.

Elias moved from this to that, "This is only ninth-century. But look at that..."

There was a pile of cuneiform tablets. "This is the library of the gods!" he said, unable to suppress his excitement.

A shelf of statues—silver foxes—captured Jamie's interest. They almost looked alive, he thought. Elias was reading from a tablet, "`The Light Ones...The Dark Ones...The Sea and Sky People'...The Dark Ones were actually the good guys, you know."

Next, Jamie found a painting that depicted dwarfs in cages being loaded onto an ancient cargo ship. And more statuettes: women with pointy hats, each holding a mask on a stick—a replica of their own faces.

"Come," Elias said. "Here are the granite anthropoid coffins." He saw that Jamie was examining a clear green stone knife.

"Take it with you," Elias said. "Come..."

Back at the camp, night was approaching and the men were chopping brushwood into bundles and feeding them into the cooking fire.

"Those are extraordinary finds," Jamie exclaimed, admiring the perfect balance of the knife he had taken.

"Just the beginning. We're close to finding a Dialer. And with that, we can turn the tide. A Dialer can do many things. And I know there's one here." Elias was getting worked up. His eyes were those of a

67

A Loud Humming Sound Came From Above

man possessed.

"Look, Jamie, it will help us in our struggle with the Committee and the Visitors who control them. I thought we might find and enlist another race, but maybe we're meant to do it all ourselves. There are records of benign Visitors in the past, but they all seem to have vanished."

"Do you think the Visitors were the gods these people worshipped, too?"

"Yes," Elias said, lighting one of the cheroots. It was an especially warm night and they decided to walk to the waterfall for some relief before dinner.

Two days later, Jamie awoke to the sound of angry voices. He peered out of his tent to see the workers confronting a larger group of natives. They were a tall, warlike tribe from the volcanic mountain who'd come down to hunt. They were known as the Ear Eaters, since a boyhood rite of passage included cutting off their right earlobe and eating it. They were armed with slick black bows and some type of throwing bolos. The leader carried a walking staff with an ape's skull as a handle and wore a faded T-shirt that advertised "The Pepsi Generation." The ancient structures that had sprouted out of the ground after the recent eruption had them in a frenzy. They were demanding to see the chief. Jamie retrieved the gun from his gear and released the safety. In the next moment, Elias appeared from out of a tomb, dressed in a fantastic, hooded robe that sparkled and flashed in the morning sunlight. He held a hoop in his hands and made a sweeping movement that produced an enormous bubble that wobbled slowly toward the natives. They threw themselves to the ground and watched it float by, speaking to each other in hushed and awed voices.

Elias approached them, speaking their language. Gradually, the natives rose to their knees. Some stood. The leader spoke a few words as well. Elias made a sign at his forehead, then a different sign at each of the other men's foreheads. He gave the chief a black leather pouch and a small golden box that brought a smile to his fearsome visage. The tribesmen turned and walked off quietly, as if they'd just been blessed by a god.

Elias strode over to Jamie's tent. "Breakfast in twenty minutes. We have a lot of work today."

Over a meal of hot oats, fruit, and tea, they watched the dark clouds moving in from the north. The workers grumbled amongst themselves.

"Looks like a harbinger, not just a storm," Elias predicted. "Let's get down there now."

As they headed back toward the structures, the first drops began to fall. As they approached the entrance to the dig, a torrential downpour was causing swamps and pools to form everywhere. Elias and Jamie were already dressed in plastic rain gear that seemed to amuse the men.

The previous day, they had opened another wall and now they were going to explore the rooms beyond it.

As the new room was being lit, they removed their rain gear. They saw more treasures but were looking for what Elias had dubbed "The War Chamber." They moved toward a row of dusty skeletons dressed in

A Loud Humming Sound Came From Above

golden helmets and breastplates, strung across a taut rope. They slid these gruesome guards aside.

They next entered a small foyer where they found a stack of horned helmets, an ivory statue of a demon the size of a child, and a box of scrolls, thin as dead skin. Elias gently lifted one of the scrolls and read a script unknown to Jamie. "Yes, yes. We're close," he said.

Next to the scrolls was a trunk of silver coins and glittering jewelry. "Trinkets," Elias said, as he pushed aside a thick curtain of black velvet, and adjusted a light that revealed another room with more artifacts. There was a golden replica of a goddess or queen, boxes of broken bones, odd weapons and implements, and a massive painting that depicted a scene of mutilation and sacrifice conducted by creatures that resembled the demon statue they'd just seen. One of the creatures was tearing flesh off a screaming child; another gnawed on a bone. The room was filled with lavish furniture, and Jamie could see now that the space was circular and even larger than he'd thought.

"Here we are," Elias said, going through the drawers of a giant armoire. He produced an illuminated map—to where, Jamie didn't know—most likely, to another lost world. And then, Elias was reading to himself from another scroll. There was an audible rumble from underground, followed by a jolt.

From the entrance, the men shouted, "Get out! The earth is falling! Come out, Mister Elias! Come out!"

"I say we stay," Elias said. "A Dialer is here. We may not have this chance again."

Other Ports, Other Hells

Jamie thought Elias could survive anything—he'd seen him live through conflicts that would kill a mortal. But even Elias had certain basic requirements, such as oxygen.

"We're looking for an old sea chest," he said calmly. "Look around. It's in this room."

A roar overhead was followed by a shifting of the room, then a shaking that felt like an earthquake. The whole underground structure began sliding into the earth, down, down, until it finally stopped. Panic seized Jamie and he wondered how much oxygen they'd have. A cold, dark fear gripped him, but he managed to pull himself out of it. He shined his flashlight around. Across the way, under a huge, dusty stack of rugs, he saw something: a chest.

"Elias! Here!"

After they pulled off the pile of rugs, Elias pried opened the lid. He brought out an apparatus that, once out of its case, reminded Jamie of an old radio, but made out of a gray metal, with three clear dials on its face. It was equipped with two sets of goggles and two thin cords. Jamie could tell from Elias's expression that this was the Dialer they sought. Elias connected the goggles and cords into the side of the thing, and clicked a switch. Somewhere inside, an electric blue light came on, accompanied by a soft hum. The dials became luminescent. "Right out of Buck Rogers," Jamie said but Elias was now totally focused.

He handed Jamie a set of goggles and uncapped the cords that connected to the Dialer on one end and exposed a small needle on the other. He inserted one needle into Jamie's leg, then the other one into his

71

A Loud Humming Sound Came From Above

own. Elias began adjusting the dials.

Jamie watched as a clear liquid traveled through the Dialer in mad circles as white light seeped out of the goggles of the two men. He saw his own eyes reflected in the goggles that Elias wore. It looked as if he and Elias were merging to survive the transport.

They found themselves beside a stream, in a thick, humid jungle. There was a burst of wind, as if provided by some benevolent god who was passing by. They removed their goggles and needles and recapped them. Jamie watched the small wound on his leg from the needle open like a flower and then disappear. Elias put the Dialer back into its leather case and strapped it onto his back. They walked off along the stream toward the sun, without speaking.

"Where are we?" Jamie finally asked.

"Somewhere..." Elias looked around and sniffed the air. "Not good. West Africa. Border of Guinea, Liberia maybe."

"Can't we use the Dialer again?"

"No." Elias lit a fresh cheroot. "We must be in a sacred place when we use it."

They made their way to the coast, riding in the backs of supply trucks past checkpoints run by teenage soldiers armed with AK-47s, gun belts crisscrossing their chests. Bizarrely, they also wore bad women's wigs, some slightly askew. When they'd approach the truck, Elias would produce a round, swirling gadget he'd picked up at the dig and mesmerize them. It instantly made the stoned little monsters trip out, their death stares dissolving into huge idiotic smiles. One, maybe thirteen years old at most, who called himself

Other Ports, Other Hells

"General Badass," got so giddy, he waved good-bye dramatically until they had driven out of sight.

In Freetown, they booked passage on a ship, the S.S. *Espirito*, headed for the Canary Islands. The ship's Master, a certain Captain Black, was one of Elias's old associates. Black was a shadowy character who favored dark glasses, a short beard, and a black fez. Once onboard his ship, he preferred a jeweled turban, a white waistcoat, and no glasses. The three of them sat in Black's cabin and sipped absinthe. The captain nodded appreciatively at the Dialer.

"I make only one quick stop at Dakar," he said. "Then it's straight sailing to Las Palmas."

"When the Conquistadores landed on the Canary Islands," Elias said, "they discovered a tribe of people called the Guanches who displayed stone tablets in a language that could not be deciphered. But the Conquistadores were not interested in such things. It's believed that they massacred the tribe, though some survived."

"There were multiple sightings of a Saturn-shaped spacecraft reported from the island in 1976," Jamie added enthusiastically.

"Aye, *Canarie Insulae*," Black intoned. "The Island of Dogs. The Dog Men. They've had contact with the Visitors."

Elias patted the Dialer. "And The Dog Men will lead us to a very sacred spot. A spot where we will take out some Committee transports, for starters."

Jamie pressed his fingertips together, practicing a finger meditation. He nodded and smiled in agreement.

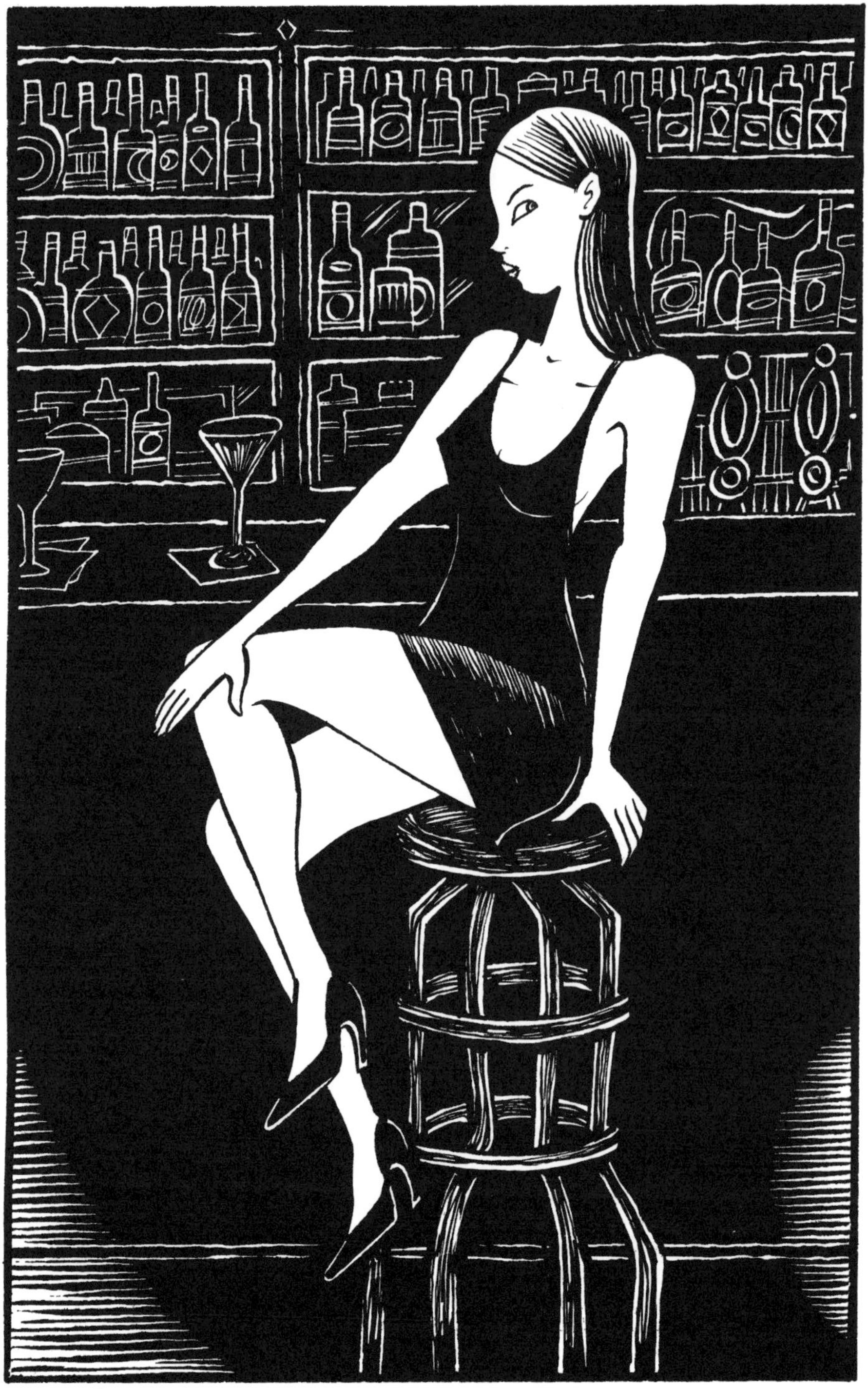

The Girl From Somewhere

SOUTHLAND

Hyde was finding it difficult to see through the bathhouse steam, and the sunblock he'd applied earlier was melting and getting into his right eye. He wiped his forehead with a towel.

Emerging from the steam was an old Japanese man. He was naked, and his expression was friendly, Hyde thought, until he noticed the knife in the man's left hand.

Hyde threw the towel into the assassin's face and stepped to the side. The old guy tripped and fell against a wall but turned again. A left kick to his arm sent the blade clattering away. Another one sent him kissing the wall as he slid to the floor. Hyde got the garrote from the pocket of his swim trunks, dropped it over the old man's neck, and tightened it. Out in the main bath area, facing the other way, was a bald guy soaking in a pool, unable to hear. But somebody could come in.

"Who sent you?" Hyde demanded.

"I cannot..."

"Then say good-bye to this world."

The old man made an ugly gagging sound but acceded with a hand signal. To anyone walking by, it might look as if they were only talking, except that the old man was on the floor, facing sideways, and Hyde was close to him. He loosened the garrote.

"M-M-Mister Appleton," the elderly man sputtered.

"Where?" Hyde demanded.

The old man pleaded with grotesque expressions rather than words. Then he gasped his last gasp, holding a throat that refused to function, and died there in front of Hyde.

Hyde removed the garrote, wondering how he could have died. It didn't make sense, but he knew it was time to leave. He hoisted him up and propped him onto the bench. Hyde picked up the knife, and turned the steam up with the wall dial. In the dressing room, he opened the guy's locker with his key and looked at his ID.

Back at the hotel where he'd checked in earlier on assignment, he called Celine.

"Hullo?"

"Hyde here. I've been tagged. Old Japanese fellow named Mishimaki sent by somebody called Appleton."

"What else?"

"That's it. He's gone. Sun Spa Steam Baths."

"Go to The Stop. You're off assignment. We'll bring you in. 1600 hours."

And with that, Celine rang off. Hyde did a sweep. The place was clean. He wondered if he'd been spotted from the street, or picked up on a remote. The Agency would find out; they found out everything, eventually.

The Girl From Somewhere

Hyde packed his case, used the service stairs, and left the rental van in the parking lot. After a taxi, a tram, a short boat ride—making sure he wasn't being tracked—Hyde arrived at the greasy hamburger diner called The Stop. He stood alone under the ratty awning.

Next door, on a decaying wall, were the remains of an advertisement for an after-hours club that was no more. Now the image was so faded, the mermaid serving a drink to a lurid-looking client looked downright haunting. Across the road, a scrubby lot of devil's grass stood shimmering under the dying sun.

A white van pulled up. Murray, the driver, wearing a white pith helmet and white jumpsuit, got out. He saluted Hyde and opened the back door. Inside, Hyde made himself a drink and sullenly watched the semi-ruined city through dark-tinted glass.

They rolled down a side road and pulled onto a lot alive with dust swirls and sat looking at four warehouses—all various shades of red. Murray escorted him to the entrance of the largest one.

They walked through a dark room and boarded an old freight elevator. Murray pressed the button for the sixth floor and the thing yawned, sighed, and groaned, then lifted them upwards. Hyde followed him through another dark room, and then a room flooded with light. They continued down an L-shaped hallway, past what looked to be a series of small medical waiting rooms, all empty, then through a vacant room that smelled faintly of dead flowers. Down a spiral staircase onto a white marble floor, and then through yet another hallway. Its walls were painted a rich, forest

A Loud Humming Sound Came From Above

green, with faintly trailing squiggles of gold and red, like an invasion of tiny jellyfish.

They arrived at a tall, ornately carved wooden door. It looked like something out of El Presidente's hacienda.

"There you go, sir," Murray said and saluted before turning and walking away.

Hyde slid his card into the slot, and the door buzzed open, revealing a deep, opulent room of dark wood, black leather club furniture, Old World artifacts, a globe, a walk-in humidor, and a wet bar. Celine sat behind an impressive desk in amber light, smoking a Corona and studying a computer screen. Hyde stepped over to the bar and made himself another drink.

"The new digs are nice," he said, and looked to see if she wanted anything, but she remained deep into whatever was on the screen.

"Okay, Hyde," she said, looking up over slim glasses. "You're out of here. Relocation. New assignment. There's a personnel van outside. It's yours. Go to El Centro. Take the picturesque drive up the coast. Take your time. We have a safe apartment for you there. Find April and get her to Black's Island. We'll meet you there."

The bourbon tasted good to Hyde and he was beginning to feel a glow. He was glad to be moving on. The work he'd been doing in Southland had become routine and boring. He'd gotten involved in a bad affair with a married woman. There was a screaming kid next door. Besides, every agent wanted to escort an April and meet the illustrious Dr. Black.

"Larry Boy will contact you and show you the

ropes up there—"

"Celine," Hyde interrupted, "I know enough to get around in that burg."

"Nonetheless, it's his domain and he insists on you at least checking in with him."

Celine mouthed the cigar and eased out a plume of blue smoke from her smallish mouth. Hyde was finding it slightly arousing, which Celine may have guessed, since she balanced the Corona on the lip of a huge ashtray, pushed her glasses up, and looked at him with a calculating demeanor.

"How did he tag me?" Hyde ventured.

"We think chance. Nori Mishimaki from Tokyo-ville was devastated by your liquidation of Dr. Ikira. Ikira was his nephew. The old man was a veteran in intelligence himself and vowed he'd kill you. He went to the Allied Asian Agency and convinced them to fund an account that would allow him to track you down." Celine stopped and slid her tongue over her front teeth.

"But he was cut off by AAA three years ago. We don't know if any information on you was leaked, but we're not taking any chances. We think it was a freak incident that he spotted you. We've checked him out. He was in Southland for only two days and was set to leave again tomorrow for Nueva York. He was here strictly on a family matter with a granddaughter in the banking business. We think he spotted you on the street and followed you to the bathhouse, as he subsequently missed the meeting he'd come here for."

"Ikira was a waste of human life. A despicable specimen, if I ever saw one. Why would...?"

A Loud Humming Sound Came From Above

"Family, Hyde. You don't understand that because you've never had any."

"The old man died strangely. I didn't kill him."

"Right. We're waiting for the autopsy. Any loose ends we should tie up for you here?"

"None at all. What about this Appleton he was muttering about?"

"The code name for his director when he was active. Died four years ago of heart failure."

EL CENTRO

Fog. Early morning. The second most bombed-out city on the West Coast. In the remains of a park, a group of slender Chinese girls were practicing Tai Chi. Although their movements created a dreamlike mood, it failed to calm Hyde. He finally started the engine and drove off. He found his new address and parked the van in its assigned garage. Inside, he found a dull room and a dull bed. He did a sweep; the place was clean. Hyde unpacked his bag and stretched out.

* * * * * * *

April's mobile phone sat on the bar and its tiny green light flickered like a beacon from some distant star.

Hyde had followed her to this bar in the wharf area: lower level, hidden, dim lighting. He sat in a booth in the back and contemplated his drink. He felt the air vibrate: April, a stylish, slinky brunette, an exotic due to a small strain of Indonesian blood, was coming back from the restroom. She eased onto a barstool.

Hyde enjoyed watching her. She wore a short skirt and crossed her legs. She let a high heel pump dangle and shifted her buttocks.

His drink had a bite and he chased it with some ice water. Monochromatic Mick entered the bar, claimed the stool next to April, and began yapping. This was the "problem" Celine had hinted at during his last briefing. Hyde wondered exactly what the relationship was, since there'd been no kiss. The couple continued to speak to one another and Hyde trailed off into a daydream that placed him already in Nueva Aires, gliding down a slow, serpentine river in a boat something like a gondola.

He was jarred back to reality by loud voices; the two were nearly yelling at each other.

"Well, fuck you, too," Monochromatic Mick snarled and stormed out of the bar, knocking over a chair.

April turned slowly toward Hyde. He stood and offered her a new seat with a grand gesture right out of an eighteenth-century French play.

"Agent Hyde, at your service."

The next afternoon, Hyde found her still asleep in his bed.

She sat up. "Is it over?"

He took her in his arms. "Well, that part is." The smell of April's hair reminded him of a summer day from long ago. Her hand crawled into his pants.

Hyde had disposed of Monochromatic Mick's body in the toxic bay where nothing was ever salvaged, and anything that did wash up had transmuted into

A Loud Humming Sound Came From Above

something like a repellent blob from some long-dead universe.

There was a video message from Larry Boy and Hyde erased it.

NUEVA AIRES

After the long hovercraft ride and a trek through a stretch of jungle, they arrived at the coast and made camp before dusk. Hyde's shirt was sweated through. April was as dry as when they'd started out. The shrieking of birds, and the croaking of frogs were an eerie accompaniment to their nocturnal activities. In the morning, as the sun came up, they watched the whirling vortexes in the high grass, caused by the circular winds. April changed the dressing on his wound caused by Monochromatic Mick's dagger stab. Later, he watched her kill a snake with a stick, almost casually. Hyde was falling for her but he realized she wasn't completely human. Maybe that was even better.

High above their camp were long-abandoned houses that one could easily miss, since the jungle had reclaimed that space with flourishing vegetation that mostly covered the structures. Hyde spotted someone on a rooftop. The figure was looking through a pair of binoculars but quickly disappeared. For a crazy moment, Hyde thought it was Larry Boy. And even later, he wasn't completely convinced that it wasn't.

They followed a map and turned away from the road, walking into the green shadow of jungle. They spent the day hiking, and by nightfall, Hyde was breathing heavily, his eyes half shut. He stood under a tree beside a pond bathed in moonlight. He plunged his knees into the mud and drank. As Hyde prepared to sleep, April watched him without expression.

They traveled all day again at a brisk pace, following a winding stream and eventually coming to a small beach. Hyde sat in the sand and drew symbols with a stick—configurations of a personal mystical significance. After removing her clothes, April began a slow dance in the sand. Soon, they were on a makeshift bed of leaves.

In the morning, April bathed. Hyde discovered a black iron bridge and walked out onto it, carefully treading the scaffolding that the workmen had left behind. He spent some time listening and watching a marsh across the way where dragonflies patrolled relentlessly.

They both smelled fire and food cooking.

That night, in a spectacular botanical garden, April took Hyde's arm. A sensation of floating backward came over him.

They looked out over a plain sprinkled with colored meteors.

They picked their way across the field and climbed a steppe. Below was the river. On amphibious crafts, dark figures walked about with acetylene torches. Laughter floated across the water. A gray, dead light dropped from the sky in the early morning.

Hyde arranged their passage on one of the crafts, and soon they were passing landscapes of junked refrigerators, washing machines, microwave ovens, and enormous piles of plastic, cardboard, and other, less definable, debris. Occasionally, they heard shouts and cries from behind the monstrous heaps. Once on the open sea, they traveled under funnel-shaped clouds and through salty sea vapors.

Midday. They reached Black's Island and were put ashore. They discovered an old stone wall, overgrown with honeysuckle, and climbed to the top. Small floating huts were moored to the banks of a calm lagoon. The scene imparted an especially curious mood, in which time seemed fragmented in shards of reflected memories.

April laughed nervously, the way people do when they're afraid or cannot understand something. Her thighs were exposed and Hyde traced them with a finger.

Finally, he would meet the infamous Dr. Black, the doctor who had designed and developed the Aprils.

"Now I am somewhere," April said softly.

A group dressed in khaki, wearing sun hats and backpacks, was coming in from a dirt road. Celine was leading with a walking stick. Murray and Larry Boy both shouldered rifles with scopes.

"I might have to do something about Larry Boy," Hyde thought.

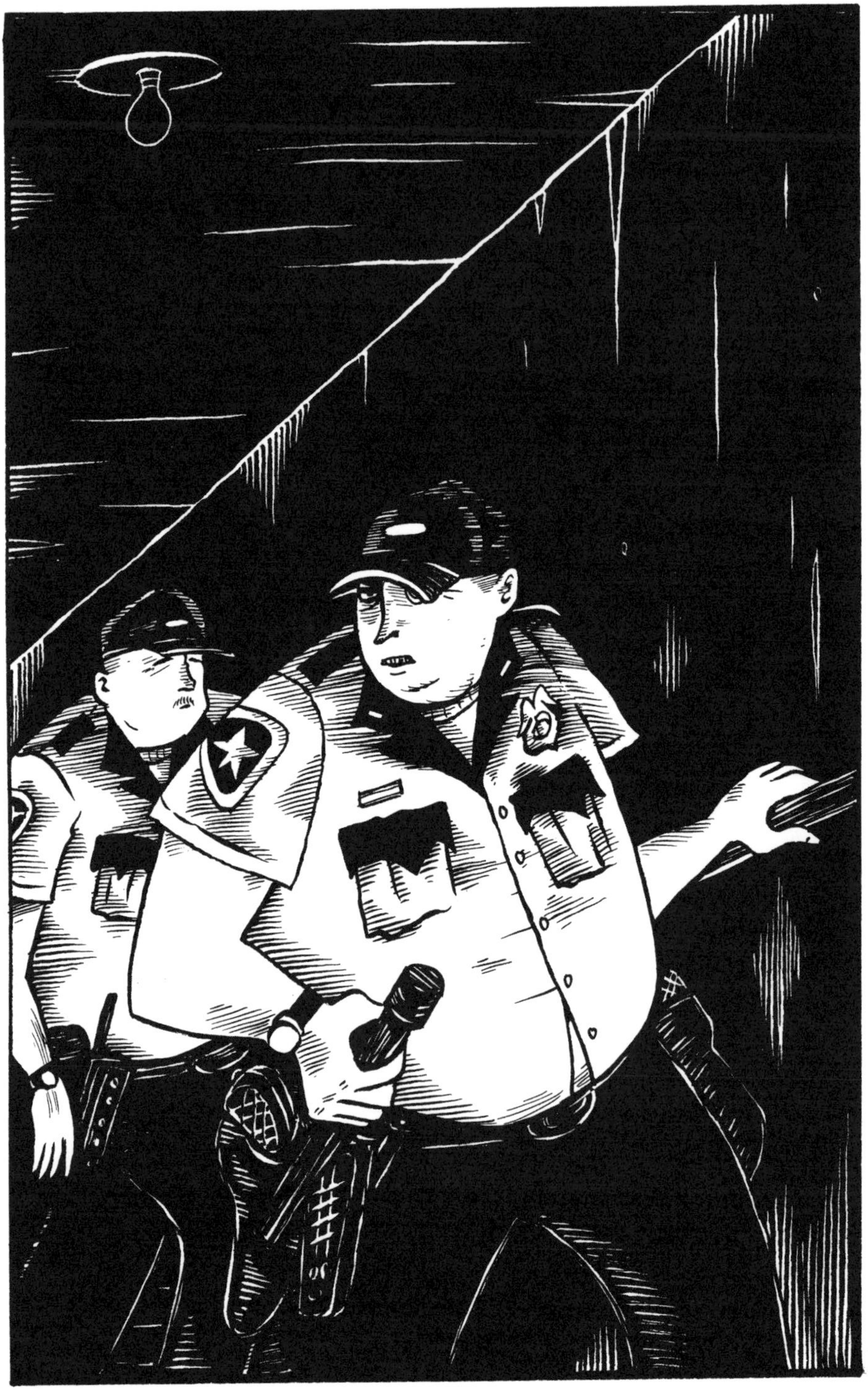

Mister Leposki

Ian was in a foul mood. His wound looked worse. It was located on his ankle and had developed from what he thought had been a spider bite. He'd scratched it open and overnight it had turned into a gaping, raw wound the size of a quarter. The pain was like an irregular biting sensation. Ian took some codeine but it didn't do much except put him into a worse mood. He hadn't taken any for months and he knew it would probably make him a little sick. When he didn't need codeine was when he generally enjoyed it: early some mornings with a strong cup of coffee, or before putting on headphones and going to work on his practice drum pads. Ian was a self-taught musician and played drums in two different bands.

Another problem was that his medical insurance (which he'd hung onto after he'd quit his job) had been discontinued due to some glitch in the system. He'd been on the phone all day with three different agencies, talking to people who seemed reluctant or unqualified to do their jobs. Eventually he was told that he would be reinstated in three days.

Ian put a large band-aid over the wound, took a few more pills, and waited for Sheryl, his on again/off again girlfriend. It was his birthday and Sheryl was

A Loud Humming Sound Came From Above

taking him out for dinner.

They chose a restaurant nearby, after he'd told her about the wound and showed it to her. "Oh gross. Ian, it's awful. You've gotta go to Emergency." He convinced her that he could wait the three days to see his regular doctor.

The meal started off with bad service and it didn't improve. "Today's the birthday of Cole Porter and Les Paul, too," Sheryl told him over coffee and dessert, trying to put a bright spot on the day.

"I bought you a present but I couldn't find it."

They both laughed. It was so typical of her.

A week later, Ian was on the phone with Sheryl. "Good news from the Wound and Burn Center. The doctor says it's looking better."

"That's great. What is it?"

"A venous ulcer."

"Hm-mm. Doesn't sound good, babe."

"Today, he used these two sticks that looked like fireplace matches. He put them on the wound and it stung like a motherfucker. They're silver nitrate or something, which cauterizes the wound and kills any bacteria. And um... I'm in what's called an Unna Boot, which is like a mummy wrap with this special silver patch on the wound. And I can't get in the shower. Anyway, it's looking better."

"What kinda boot?"

"Unna. An Unna boot. Like a mummy."

One year, Ian had spent a month in Puerto Angel, Mexico, as a base for surfing, fishing, and scuba diving activities. He'd met an interesting older man staying at the same posada. The man was a well-seasoned

Mister Leposki

traveler, ex-seaman, and ex-pot smuggler. He was there working on his memoirs.

If one wasn't careful in Puerto Angel—hell, almost any part of Mexico, really—one could get freaky sick eating or drinking the wrong thing. It'd only happened to Ian once, and it was entirely his fault: a questionable seafood pasta at one of the funky beach hut restaurants. He'd stayed in his cabin for two days, sicker than he could ever remember. Finally, he wandered out and down a hot, dusty road, stopping at a roadside stand and guzzling two bottles of Coca Cola straight down. Nothing had ever tasted better. The Indian vendor smiled from behind the counter of her wooden stand. It still took him a few more days before his regular appetite returned. His new friend laughed about it and said, "Man, you shot yourself in the foot. Don't eat anything at those joints. The stuff sits there all day." But even he got sick on a side trip to Oaxaca City when he gambled on a *licuado* from a street stand.

One morning at the posada's communal breakfast, he sat Ian down and said, "I can guarantee you that neither of us will get sick again down here." He began to cut up bulbs of raw garlic on a wooden cutting board. "Take what you think you can handle," he said, and Ian swallowed a small pile. They and a few others did this every morning, and nobody who partook got sick again.

Ian loved garlic anyway: he roasted it and cooked with it, but he hadn't eaten it raw since that trip. Then he watched a TV show all about garlic and its many benefits. It was supposed to aid blood circulation as

A Loud Humming Sound Came From Above

well as work as a natural antibiotic. He decided to start eating it raw again, with his breakfast. Taken in the right spirit, there would be no garlic breath, claimed one expert. Chewing up some parsley afterward was recommended by others. The first thing he noticed was a boost in his energy that lasted most of the day. The next thing he noticed was a healthy hard-on.

Ian waited for the bus that would take him to Sheryl's. The first one was so packed, he decided to wait for the next. He felt queasy just considering the prospect of getting on an overcrowded bus. He'd just taken a few bong hits and needed some room. The next bus had only a few passengers, and he climbed aboard. Ian watched a hillbilly-looking dude standing by the back door jerking his head like a chicken.

The hillbilly yelled out, "Back door!" but too late, and the bus kept moving. When it pulled over at the next stop, the hillbilly got out, but not before yelling "Pig shit!" Everybody cracked up except the driver, a stone faced black man.

Sheryl, who worked as an exotic dancer, was getting ready for work and not in the mood for lovemaking. Ian could have insisted but, instead, he went into the kitchen and made himself a chicken salad sandwich. He sat at the kitchen table and ate, had a cup of coffee, and read the paper.

Sheryl, looking more like she was going to the gym than a strip club, except for her dramatic make-up, came into the kitchen and poured herself a cup.

"How would you like to take a trip to Mexico?" Ian asked, putting an arm around her waist.

Mister Leposki

She laughed. "Sure, who's paying for it?"

"Who do you think?"

"Listen, honey, I wanna tell you about a client I had last night who really creeped me out. And he's supposedly a friend of Mr. Leposki's."

The black Ford Crown Victoria appeared out of the fog. Searchlights were mounted on each side of the car. Decals on the doors depicted a pyramid and a badge, though one had to look closely to see that it was a badge—at a glance, it looked more like a pineapple. Large block letters across the trunk read: SECURITY. The car pulled in and stopped in front of a weathered high-rise that looked more like a prison from a bleak future. The two men inside the car were dressed in gray-and-black uniforms. They were both armed with .357 Magnums. The men looked straight ahead as they spoke; muted squawk voices on the radio called out unintelligible messages. The driver, 34-year-old Leo, said: "That was some meeting huh? Security from the Mallers, Office Inc., Airport, hell even the Nuke boys were there this time."

"Yeah," Monty agreed. "We're gonna have one hell of a union."

Monty was ten years Leo's senior and smarter, yet Leo was his superior. "What d'ya think of the secrecy, though?" Monty asked. "And the weird swearing-in ceremony?"

"I think it's the shit. Very Skull-and-Bones."

"Yeah, it is kinda cool, huh?"

"Tonight's a priority," Leo stated, looking at a printout on his clipboard. "Pick up and deliver a Ms. Sheryl Owens, also known as 'Sunshine.'" Monty

A Loud Humming Sound Came From Above

began arranging some crystal meth on a mirror.

"Later, we need to check the fence back at the compound, and check out some possible unauthorized drug dealing by the new mechanic. But first, and very foremost, this cunt," he nodded toward the building, then snorted the two lines that Monty had passed him.

The men got into the building easily; a tenant leaving figured they were the real thing. The elevator was broken, so they climbed to the 12th floor, carrying night sticks that doubled as electric prods. Monty carried a case of tools. They were flying on the speed and looking forward to picking up the dancer and scaring her some, before delivering her to Mr. Leposki. They pounded on the door with the butts of their batons.

Ian and Sheryl were in her unmade bed, Sheryl's legs atop Ian's shoulders. Ian was fucking her with a steady rhythm that matched the banda beat leaking from the kitchen radio. The loud knocks distracted him and he looked at Sheryl, whose makeup was now messy enough to make her appear slightly crazy. "F-f-forget it, honey. I'm not expecting ah...anyone—"

The banging got louder. Sheryl climbed off and started angrily for the door when Ian grabbed her and pulled her back. She looked at him funny as he worked a trouser leg over his wrapped ankle.

"Is my gun still in the drawer?"

She looked confused, then fearful. "Sure it is. Where you left it. But..."

There was a new sound now—a drill. They both knew that whoever was behind that door was coming

Mister Leposki

in, and with malicious intent. Sheryl sat behind the bed on the floor, against the wall, and tried to stop herself from shaking. Ian found his gun, checked the clip, released the safety, and assumed his firing stance.

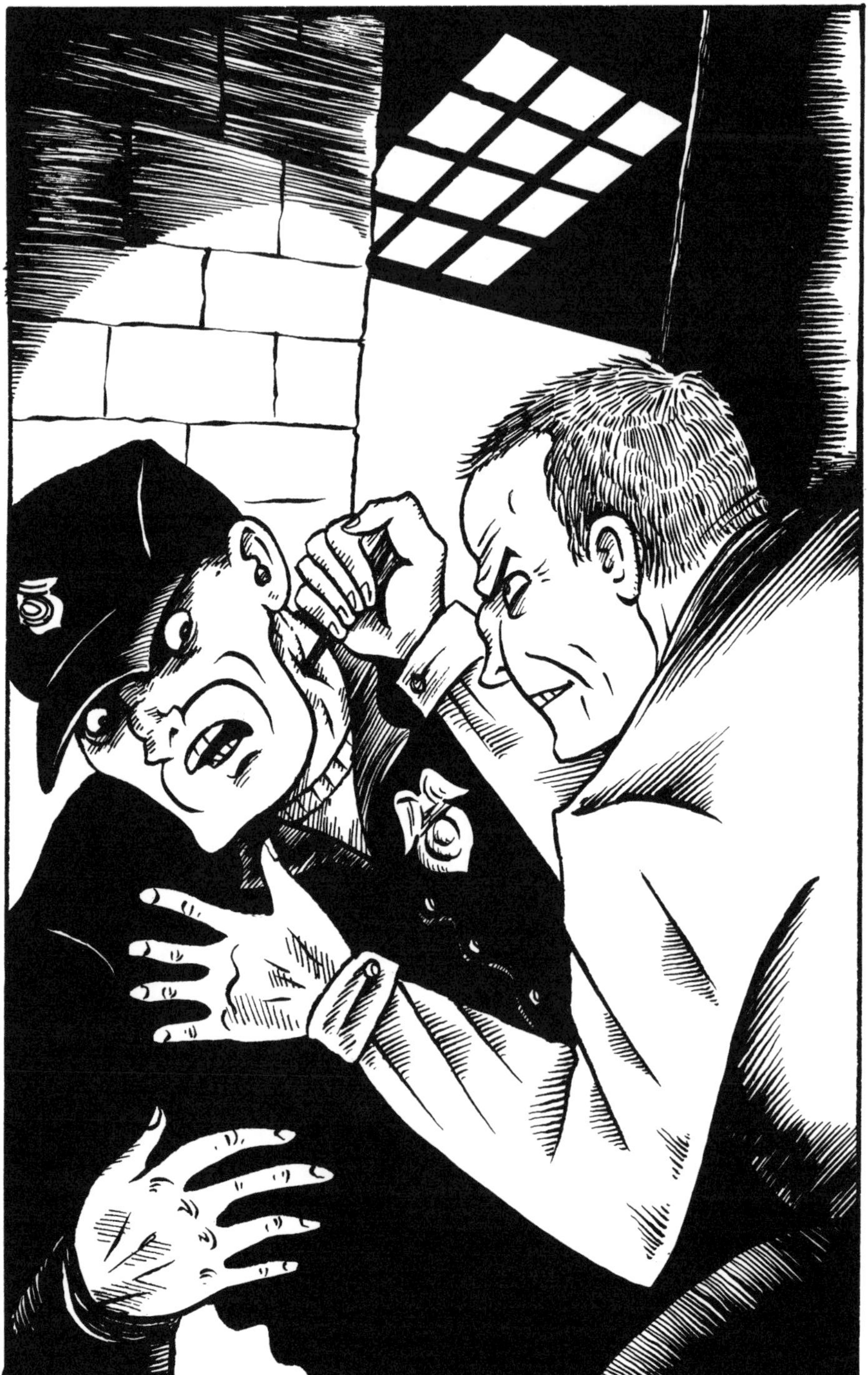

Lady Killer

There was a mix-up with the paperwork. Even the furlough captain had missed it when he'd stamped all the forms. A light-blue laminated "Inmate Activity Card" with the warden's childlike signature was paper-clipped to the top of the file.

Later that morning, an older trustee handed the card and a pink slip of paper through the bars to Brendan Cattrell, a.k.a. "Baby Face Cattrell," before winking lewdly and trotting away. Cattrell laughed. Yes, he still had the charm.

Dumbfounded, Baby Face sat on his bunk and looked it over. "Brendan Cattrell is authorized to participate in scullery work at an undisclosed outside location." Cattrell had just been transferred from maximum security Pelican Bay prison, and he was thrilled to his core with this colossal mistake.

The next morning, dressed in his prison-issued striped jacket and gray cap, he waited until two bulls showed up with five other prisoners in tow. A guard unlocked the cell and placed him in cuffs. The group was led down one prison hallway after another, picking up more prisoners, solid metal gates slamming shut and locking behind them. Baby Face told himself that if he could just relax, this would be his greatest escape—one for which the prison system itself would be responsible. He wanted to laugh out loud but, instead, stared at the floor in front of him.

Baby Face boarded an old bus with twenty-two other prisoners. Ten minutes later, the bus was rolling down a country road, away from the prison, across a sea of open fields. The fog made the landscape look like Sleepy Hollow. Before long, the bus turned onto a wider highway and then onto a freeway. The handcuffs would have to come off at some point, Cattrell mused. He gazed at the morning traffic, trying to imagine where people were going and what they were doing in their lives. He would soon be with them. Baby Face concentrated on keeping his heartbeat steady and his mind in a quiet space. He looked at the activity card again. He was number 1640. Added together, that made eleven. That was his lucky number. Added again made two. He was born in February, the second month. The numbers were lining up nicely.

The bus took a turnoff and began to rumble down an industrial road that was also thick with fog. He could make out white buildings, some kind of a metal tower, tractors, cement mixers, a row of pale green portatoilets. The bus kept rolling, the fog dissipated, and eventually the beginnings of the city outskirts were evident: a grocery store, dilapidated housing, weedy fenced-in lots, graffiti-covered walls, a gloomy gas station. The bus pulled into a parking lot behind a three-story warehouse the color of red clay, and parked near an open loading dock.

"Stay in your seats!" the bull barked from the front of the bus. "I'll tell ya when you can move. And

Lady Killer

keep your cards in front of you at all times!" He shot a menacing glance at the prisoners before getting off the bus. The driver rustled the morning paper and began to read it. Somebody farted loudly and a general complaint rose up from the men that caused the bull to climb back onboard and command, "Silence, you fucks!" Then he said something to the driver before turning back to the prisoners.

"When I call your name, get your sorry ass up and off the bus. You'll be escorted to the workplace where you'll work till chow. Understood?" The prisoners grumbled a "yes, sir" in unison and the bull called out the first name: "Sanders, front and center."

Cattrell craned his neck to see the prisoner being escorted by another bull into the entrance. His cuffs were still on. The escape would have to be from the inside. He waited for his name, still worried that someone would discover the mistake that had gotten him this far.

"Okay, Cattrell. Let's go."

Two bulls glared up at him as he stepped out of the bus, and one pointed him toward the short climb to the loading zone where a city cop stood sucking his lips. Down a couple of hallways—not so different from the prison, sans clanking metal doors—as the cop and a bull traded comments about a baseball game. Suddenly, he was looking into a deep room with a ceiling nearly as high as a cathedral, crowded with prisoners busy scrubbing pots and pans, loading and unloading dishwashers, filling plastic trays with clean dishes, glasses and little metal dessert cups, and stacking the trays on dollies. The enormous room was

A Loud Humming Sound Came From Above

filled with steam and noise and sweat and a sense of hellish boredom. A man with crazy, blue eyes, wearing a camouflage bill cap, left the working horde to snatch Cattrell's Activity Card and look into his eyes with sullen hate. He nodded to the bull, who was removing Cattrell's cuffs.

"How's it goin', Stu?" he asked the guard.

"It's alright. Here's another slave."

Crazy Eyes laughed and studied Cattrell like an insane drill sergeant.

"I want grease, chump. Elbow grease. Time's a wastin', lady." He led Cattrell over to some sinks filled with what looked like near-boiling water. An ugly pan coated with dark slime floated on top. Baby Face removed his cap and jacket. Next to the sink, a stack of cruddy pans of various shapes and sizes rose to the height of a short man—no, make that a short woman, Cattrell thought. Crazy Eyes handed him a pair of blue rubber gloves and winked, "To keep yer hands nice and soft." Then, "Do it! Now!"

Cattrell dug in, scrubbing at the pan with a bristle brush, but it was so thick with gluey gravy that Cattrell felt there was no possibility of the pan ever being clean again. He gave up, filled it with some of the boiling water, and placed it on the floor. The next one he tried seemed more promising and, after a few minutes of scrubbing, showed signs that it might actually be cleaned in his lifetime. Cattrell worked away but kept scanning the room, observing and noting the general set-up. Behind him was a new guard, and on the other side of the room stood two more watching the deep cavern like a pair of vultures.

Lady Killer

Baby Face turned around and looked at the guard behind him sipping coffee from a styrofoam cup. The bull stepped closer and said, "What's the problem? Get back to work." Baby Face pleaded that he had to use the bathroom. He held his legs together and made the most pathetic expression he could muster. The guard laughed at his discomfort and took another sip. He narrowed his eyes and sipped again. "There's a piss break coming up soon," he said, but then saw that Cattrell was in a bad way. "Okay, son, come with me," the guard said, and Baby Face peeled off the gloves. In the hallway, they stopped in front of the men's room. The guard said, "I've gotta put the cuffs back on." Cattrell went back into his leg-squeezing pose and pained expression. The guard still had his coffee. He thought for a moment, then said, "Okay, go ahead. I'll come with you."

The bathroom was empty. There were no windows. Cattrell turned to the urinal and unzipped. He slipped out a brush handle with a jagged piece of metal from a dessert dish imbedded into it and wrapped tight with a shoestring. He had contrived the weapon under the hot dishwater, which ended up making it weld together nicely. The guard lit a cigarette and the smell was almost intoxicating to Baby Face as he went ahead and urinated.

As soon as he finished, Cattrell turned and leapt like a wild animal at the guard, savagely plunging the shiv into his throat and twisting it around. As he fell, the guard made gasping sounds, and tried to kick Cattrell off while he groped for his gun, but in a matter of seconds Baby Face had finished him off with a vicious

A Loud Humming Sound Came From Above

kick to the head. He bolted the door, washed up, and got the guard's dark trousers off. He pulled them over his own jail stripes. He took his bloody prison-issued shirt off, settling for only a white t-shirt. He took stock of his newly acquired items: loaded revolver, fat wallet, pack of Camel filters, Zippo lighter, set of cuffs, and keys. He picked up the lit cigarette and took a drag. He dropped it back on the floor and stepped on it. He stood on the sink and knocked out the air vent cover above. After he had raised himself inside and closed up the vent, he crawled along a narrow air shaft like a human worm, trying not to breathe too deeply; there was a vague smell of burning plastic. At the next opening, he removed the vent cover and peered down into an empty room of lockers and benches.

Once inside the room, he found a smelly, red sweatshirt, which he put on, and even a pair of sunglasses, which he propped on his head. He let himself out and walked the hallway looking for an exit. He passed a man in a suit and another in a chef's outfit deep in a heated discussion; neither seemed even cognizant of him. Still, he kept a firm grip on the gun in the pouch of the sweatshirt. Outside, he found himself in a parking lot with a city street just beyond it. He crossed the lot and became a "free man," walking along a block of East Oakland. He turned a corner, then another, and boarded a bus.

Baby Face Cattrell came from Chicago and didn't know Oakland or San Francisco. He had been to California only twice: once as a boy, on vacation with his foster family in San Diego, where he'd almost drowned. Still, he remembered the pretty boats, and

Lady Killer

now arriving at Jack London Square, he found boats there, too. Some looked like yachts. His second time in California was when he had traveled to Sacramento for the "job."

Once off the bus, he bought a gray sweater, and ditched the red sweatshirt in a men's room trashcan. He walked until he came to a BART station and bought a ticket to San Francisco. He enjoyed the smooth ride and got out at Embarcadero, the first Frisco stop. He walked along Market Street, relishing the reality of his third escape. He needed some ID and then to head south of the border, but first he felt he deserved some fun. Looking at the *San Francisco Chronicle* in the vending machines he passed, he was reminded: it was New Year's Eve. How appropriate, he thought, and pondered if perhaps there was some even deeper meaning.

Baby Face sat in a restaurant and ate a "breakfast burrito." He had never heard of it but had watched the counterman make one: scrambled eggs, potatoes, cheese, salsa, bacon, and refried beans. He was nearly salivating as it was handed to a friendly girl standing next to him. "I'll have the same," he told the arrogant-appearing counterman. He overheard the girl order a "Mango Monkey" at the next counter, but he decided he would just have a cup of coffee.

Now satisfied, he sat at the counter and wondered what the night—New Year's Eve, no less—might hold in store for him. Outside, he lit a cigarette and took a deep hit, then dropped it to the ground and stepped on it, as was his custom. A homeless man, who looked like an extra from a Dickens epic, dropped

A Loud Humming Sound Came From Above

to his knees, retrieved the fag, straightened it out, and exposed a horrible, toothless grin.

At a bar, Baby Face found an envelope on the floor that contained a ticket to the Golden Gate Yacht Club's New Year's Eve party. He had a few drinks and decided to go. Once at the yacht club, he had a few more. He met a flirty and tipsy "Miss Royale" by the punch bowl. She wore a pink-and-black striped satin corset; black elbow-length gloves; a silver bracelet above one elbow; and a purple flower in her dark hair. Her painted face was as fetching as any harlot dreamed up by any newly escaped, baby-faced, lady killer. He smiled his special smile, the one that always worked. He watched with pleasure as her pupils enlarged.

"You're the most beautiful doll in all the world," he whispered with a sweet, deathly sincerity. Miss Royale nearly swooned. He offered his arm; she eagerly grasped it, and they left the yacht club together.

* * * * * * *

The sky threatened rain and Cattrell felt a cold wind kicking up. A clump of white balloons was caught on the electric cables of the bus line. The sidewalk before him was sprinkled with glitter, confetti, a smashed noisemaker.

He watched the attendants wheel the stretcher out of the apartment building. The corpse was covered with a white sheet.

He fished out a cigarette, lit it, took one drag, and dropped it to the ground. He looked down and stepped on it.

Lady Killer

Baby Face Cattrell thought about his next move. He still needed proper ID to get him to Mexico. He knew someone in San Diego who could supply it. He headed to the bus station and bought a ticket. He found a darkened area in an empty waiting room. He slunk into one corner and, on a hard wooden bench, dozed off behind a *San Francisco Examiner*.

When Baby Face awoke, he found that the terminal was deserted. There was not a soul in sight. He didn't feel well, either. He walked around looking for someone but he was completely alone. Spooked now, he desperately wanted to get out, but all the doors were locked. He smashed a glass door with a trashcan; the foul-smelling air rushed in and Baby Face gasped and clutched at his throat. He fell to the floor, his chest contracting with a nightmare force. He struggled to crawl across the grimy floor but he didn't know where he was crawling to. He felt the blood rushing up his throat and he thought his heart was exploding, silently, profoundly; and then he died. Two men in biohazard suits and gas masks hurried by, barely glancing at Baby Face Cattrell's lifeless body.

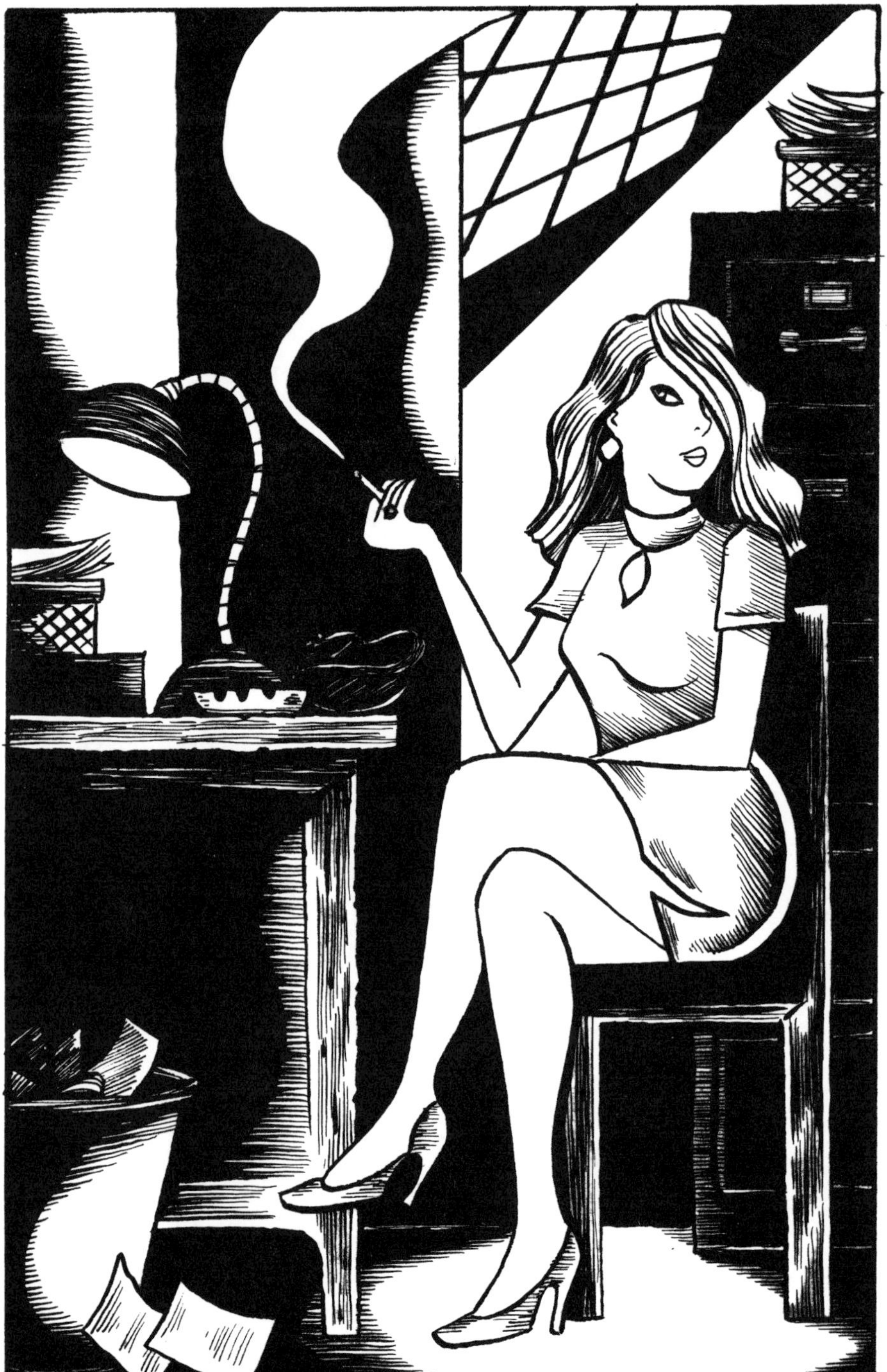

BOILED IN MIAMI

All of my adult life, I've been getting the same line: "Dan Roscoe? Why, that sounds like a private eye." Well, guess what, pal? I *am* a private eye.

I'm located in Miami, near the famous Coconut Grove, where I almost never venture, except for a stroll to the docks some nights when it's too damned hot to sleep. Early one morning, I received a breathy call that made my mind wander. Topaz Tanning said she needed my help and wanted to come over right away.

"I can't talk about it on the phone," she said. I told her to stop by in an hour.

As I was finishing a scotch neat, I heard a car pulling into the gravel driveway. I peeked out the blind to see a shapely blonde stepping out of a red Jaguar. She looked around. I was at the screen door when she arrived on my porch.

"Dan Roscoe?" she asked, from behind red-tinted star-shaped sunglasses.

"That would be me. Please come in, Miss Tanning."

She extended a perfectly manicured hand with a topaz ring I could've choked on.

"Have a seat," I said, removing a newspaper and a plastic bag from the best chair in the room. She sat

A Loud Humming Sound Came From Above

and crossed her legs—tan, shapely legs. She removed her sunglasses, revealing Barbie Doll eyes as blue as a Caribbean lagoon. I sat behind my old, steel desk and fiddled with a sharpened pencil.

"Alrighty, Ms. Tanning. What can I do for you?" I asked, poised to make some notes.

"Call me Topaz. And the first thing you can do is give me a good fuck."

I snapped my pencil point and my jaw dropped. She laughed.

"That was just to break the ice," she said. "I know the effect I have on men." I nodded and picked up another pencil. She smiled. "I will have one of those," she motioned toward the friendly, green bottle of J&B. I poured her one and another for myself.

After a sip, Topaz turned serious: "Mr. Roscoe, I think I'm in danger of being murdered. I broke off an affair a few months back with someone I believe is connected with organized crime. I think I'm being followed." She tossed down her drink and I refilled her glass. "He said if I ever left him, he'd have me killed." There was an audible choke in her voice at the end of that declarative sentence. She dug into her pocketbook and came up with a pack of Eve Lights. She lit one with a jeweled lighter and inhaled.

"Do you think you were followed here?"

"I don't know." She exhaled smoke out her pretty nose. "I don't think so."

"Have you been to the police?"

"Yes. They filed a report and stopped by a couple nights, but I got the feeling they were...well, just humoring me."

Boiled In Miami

"Have you considered moving?"

"Yes, but I figure he'd track me down." She sipped scotch and crossed her legs again.

"Well, what makes you think he's followed you? And that he'd actually go through with something a lot of unhinged, obsessed men might say after a steamy affair with the likes of you?"

I tried to pour her another drink but she covered the glass with her hand.

"Well, first, there's the phone calls," she said, "even though I've had my number changed. It's always the same voice—a man with a lisp who says, 'I'm still wathing you.' Sometimes he laughs, and it's a frightening laugh. I used to curse him, but now I hang up, pour a drink, and pop a couple of pills. And then there's the *feeling*." Topaz gave me a funny look. "I can feel someone looking, maybe even filming or photographing me. And I've had awful dreams about someone with a huge knife."

"Are you still in touch with Mister...?"

"Hoffman, Marty Hoffman. No, not at all. After I broke it off, he called and left a ton of messages—begging, pathetic messages and arrogant, hostile ones. Then he'd call and hang up. Finally he left one last message with a lot of *fuck yous*. He's too smart to say he'd kill me on a phone machine."

Topaz scrunched out her cigarette in my Little Havana ashtray. "Besides your usual fees, I'll give you a bonus to stop him."

I got out my standard contract. She fished around in her bag for her checkbook. I told her to go back to her place in South Beach and stay put, and that I'd see her again that afternoon.

As she left, I eyed her again through the blinds. This time, she didn't look around: she just climbed into her car, and started the engine. As Topaz pulled away, I spotted the neighborhood brat crossing the lot with a small bow and a quiver of arrows on his back. The other day I'd seen him throwing rocks at a couple of the feral cats until his father dragged him away. As the red Jaguar disappeared, I watched the kid walk back behind a vacant building. I finished my drink, locked the door, and headed out.

At the vacant building, I peered around the corner. The kid was eyeing a cat asleep in the sun, and reaching back for an arrow. I picked up a nice throwing rock, did my old college wind-up, and aimed at the kid's side as if it were a strike zone.

"Oof, owwww!" he yelled when the rock struck. The cat shot out of sight. The kid doubled over and dropped his bow. He sat on the ground holding his side, looking like he was going to cry or scream. He did a little of both.

I stepped back out of sight and yelled, "Leave the fucking cats alone!" Then I walked off down the street with the morning crowd, heading for my car, which was getting an oil change nearby.

Marty Hoffman owned and managed La Felecia, an old-style Italian restaurant on Collins Avenue. It wasn't open yet, so I bought a *Miami Herald* and stopped at a bar across the street. I ordered a beer. I browsed a piece about a young mother who had drowned her kids and then had gone dancing at a disco. I had finished my second beer when I saw the doors of the restaurant swing open. A huge man wearing a black suit and a white apron stepped out, blinking in the sunlight. He lit a cigarette. The guy looked like an ex-boxer with a face even a mother might be reluctant to love. I crossed the street and approached the lug, who gave me a glare, then a half smile when I asked him what the specials were for the day.

"Everything is special," he said, flicking a half-smoked butt into the street, just missing a skinny guy with blue hair and a silver helmet who zipped by on roller blades.

"Do you like fish?" he asked.

"Well sure, as long as it's not gagging on mercury."

He didn't like my answer and gave me a dark look. "We only serve fresh fish," he stated. "We have a very nice sea bass today sautéed in oil and garlic, and it's served with polenta or pasta and fresh asparagus."

"Well, that does sound good," I said. "But it's still a little early for me. Listen, Marty wouldn't be around, would he?" Something funny happened with the guy's eyes: they went all steely, and then he looked at me closer.

"Who you with?" he asked in an intimidating manner.

"I'm with nobody. I'm a private investigator and would like to talk with Marty about a personal matter." The giant thought about that for a moment and then invited me in. The interior was like a *Godfather* set and empty except for an old-timer behind the bar slicing limes. The waiter motioned toward a chair and I took it. He was back in few minutes with a lopsided smile I

A Loud Humming Sound Came From Above

didn't particularly care for.

"Follow me," he said. We went into a back area past coat racks, some public phones, restrooms, and finally to a black metal door. The giant nodded toward the door and headed off in the direction of the john. I knocked and a voice said to come in. Behind a desk similar to my own sat a handsome, middle-aged man who stood and offered a hand and a smile.

"Marty Hoffman. What can I do for you?" He gestured toward a chair. We sat and I told him who I was and who my client was.

"Alright," he said. "What's the problem?"

I laid out the scenario. Marty listened and his expression went from curiosity to concern. When I was finished, he lit a cigarette. The barkeep came in and served us each a mug of beer.

"First, I have no mob connections," Marty said after drinking off half of his brew. "Oh, I casually know a couple of wiseguys who dine here on occasion, but they don't even give me tips on the dog races. I probably bragged to Topaz about knowing those guys. Yeah, I was upset when she broke it off. But once I had some time on my own, I decided it was for the best. She's a knockout, as you know. But there's other baggage, that, uh, I won't go into 'cos it's personal. But anyway, I decided that it'd been fun but definitely wasn't meant for the long term."

"The caller says 'I'm wathing you,'" I repeated.

"I don't know anyone with a speech impediment. Don't have a clue who that could be."

I finished my beer, wound up my talk with Marty, and gave him my card. On the way out, Vic Damone was singing "You Were Only Fooling." The waiter was nowhere in sight—probably still on the crapper. The bartender was having a little nip.

Earlier I'd called a friend with the South Beach Police: Robert O'Connell in Criminal Investigations. I drove over to the main station on Washington Avenue and found a parking space after driving around for ten minutes. At the front entrance, a gang of motorcycle cops wearing short sleeves and shades sat on their bikes, talking.

Inside, the desk sergeant, a sullen, square-jawed guy with a band-aid on his neck, told me to have a seat while he called Detective O'Connell. A few moments later, O'Connell came out and gestured for me to follow him to his office. O'Connell was near my age, around thirty, with red hair, green eyes, and wearing a tie covered with happy faces that probably had been a gift. I told him about the case and my visit with Marty Hoffman, while he felt a spot on his chin that he'd missed shaving. He did some keyboarding on a laptop, stopped, opened a drawer, and produced a bottle of Early Times. O'Connell poured us each a belt into a couple of cloudy glasses.

"No mob. No nothing," he said. "Hoffman is clean." He punched some more keys, then studied the screen some more. "No record of domestic violence. Not even a friggin' parking ticket. No, wait—there *is* something...minor altercation in front of a queer bar. Guy whistled at Hoffman. He gave the guy a black eye. No charges. Settled out of court. But yeah, I do remember Topaz Tanning. Who wouldn't? We watched her place for a while but there was no activity. Whattya think, Dan?"

"Oh, maybe she's got some sorry stalker who harasses her and then backs off. She's a woman to try even a sane man's disposition."

"Yeah, one of those honeys who just oozes the stuff, eh?" O'Connell winked, looked at his bourbon, and finished it. I finished mine too.

"Well, thanks for checking. And for the drink."

"No problemo, Dan. Anytime. And if you nail this nut, call us quick."

Now I was hungry, but not in the mood for oily sea bass with a giant leering at me. There was a Cuban restaurant I liked, not far from the beach. I headed in that direction.

After lunch, I tried to finish up the paper but it was a hard read: "Grisly find in suburban Florida home...mummified bodies of a woman, son, dog..." I tossed it aside, punched in Topaz's number on my cell, and she picked up right away. I told her I'd be over within a half-hour.

Topaz Tanning's house wasn't far—a left turn on 20th, inland almost to Dade Boulevard. I pulled into the driveway and looked down a declining, grassy hillside that ended at a pool glistening in the midday heat. The house was French Colonial style. I could see part of a garage in the back.

An S-shaped walkway of rose-colored flagstone led to the front door. I pressed the doorbell button; I didn't hear it ring, but a few moments later, the door swung open to a tall, bald guy with beady eyes and a thin mouth. He was wearing a butler's uniform, of sorts: a dark jacket—too small—and a yellow tie. His slacks were black-and-white checked chef pants—also a bad fit. In his mismatched outfit, he reminded me of a vaudeville comedian, but with an aura of brutishness. I introduced myself.

"Madame will see you in the sun room, Mr. Roscoe," he said in a surprisingly pleasant voice, making a sweep with his arm. "Straight ahead, sir."

I found "Madame" lounging with her shoes off on a velvet couch having a cocktail. On a tray before her were glasses, olives, toothpicks, and a tall shaker of martinis. She said hello and motioned for me to help myself. I did and took in the opulent room that looked out onto a patio filled with flowers.

"Who's your butler?" I asked, and tried to pour her another.

"Ivan is more than my butler," she said, covering her glass. "He does...well, a lot."

"He looks like he could offer protection as well."

"Yes, but he's not that bright, and I have him busy all the time, anyway. But, yes, his presence gives me some comfort."

I told Topaz about my conversations with Marty and Detective O'Connell, and my conclusion that she was probably dealing with a stalker who might be dangerous—not just annoying. Topaz chewed on a gin-soaked olive and thought about it. She asked if I would stay in the guesthouse above the garage for a few nights. I said sure, but that I'd have to go back to Coco for a few things.

At my apartment, I threw a bag together and loaded a few other items into the car. As I was finishing up, Ralph, a nosy old geezer from next door, came

A Loud Humming Sound Came From Above

over with something on his mind.

"Hey, did ya hear about the kid?"

"What kid?"

"Ya know, the little shit that runs around here throwing rocks? Dicky Coleman? Dirty Dicky?"

"What about him?"

"Oh, he got some of his own medicine, I reckon. Somebody hit him with a rock and it caused some internal bleeding or something and they rushed him over to Mercy."

"Well, that's a shame," I said, wanting to get on my way.

"Going on a little trip?" Ralph asked.

"A very little trip. Just a few days in SoBe on a case. Well, gotta go, Ralph."

I punched in the number for Mercy Hospital on my cell. I gave the switchboard operator the brat's name and, after a couple of clicks and beeps, I got a ring and a little boy's voice answered: "Hello?"

"Leave the fucking cats alone." I said.

There was dead silence, then he screamed, "Mommy!" I guess she was there in the room. I hung up. Back on the causeway, the lights of Miami's skyline twinkled in the sultry evening. I sipped from my flask and laughed.

The guesthouse above the garage was splendid. I stretched out on the king-size bed and flipped channels on the large-screen TV. Topaz would phone if anything unusual happened or if she got another call from the creep. I had a nightcap, turned in early, and left my cell phone on a stand next to the bed.

In the morning, there were a couple of knocks at

Boiled In Miami

the door. I looked out to see Ivan bearing a breakfast tray and a single white rose in a little cut-glass vase. I let him in and he set the table, handed me a linen napkin, and let himself out. I covered the waffles and fruit medley with the napkin. I dumped the glass of water into the sink but saved the ice cubes and poured some scotch over them. I called Topaz and told her I was going to take a look around the neighborhood. She wanted to know if I'd be back by ten, since she planned to sunbathe and swim. I said I'd be back by ten; I knew I didn't want to miss that.

On my walk around the neighborhood, I found the usual: art galleries, boutiques, a vintage clothing store, a bakery, a gas station. I also spotted a spooky Haitian restaurant. Coming down the street toward me were three adult men with Down syndrome being minded by a middle-aged Hispanic woman and a flashy, young Hispanic man with a camera around his neck. The male caretaker looked out of place with his headband, baggy rapper clothing, gold chains, and mustache. The Down syndrome trio was led by a Caucasian male with gray hair who kept closing his eyes and rubbing them. Behind him was a Negro who stared gloomily at the ground. The third was another male Cauc, short, with an expression as though he were witnessing a mind-boggling scene wherever he looked. He'd occasionally wander off from the pack and the male caretaker would steer him back and say something to him. As they passed near me, heading toward the bakery, the little guy wandered off again. The minder herded him back and warned: "Stay put, Billy. I'm wathing you."

A Loud Humming Sound Came From Above

Bingo.

The caretakers and their three charges finally came out of the bakery and walked back in the direction they'd come from. I followed them and, after a few blocks, they headed into a white stucco house surrounded by a yard that needed mowing a month ago. A plaque on the front door read: ASA, Advocates of Special Adults; it listed a phone number and the director's name. I wrote it all down.

At 9:30 A.M., I called Topaz and told her I was onto something and would be back as soon as I could. In the meantime, I asked her to write down the names of all the organizations that she'd made donations to in the last two years. She started to complain, but finally agreed. I heard her calling for Ivan as she hung up the phone.

When I got back to her place, I took the list Topaz handed me and checked it, sitting at her small writing desk. Sure enough, there was ASA, twice.

"Well?" she asked, standing above me in a red bikini.

"I'm still working on it," I said. "Go back to the pool and enjoy yourself. I'll be close by."

I set up a chair in the shade alongside the guesthouse and opened a long leather case I'd brought with me. I was hidden from sight yet still had a good view of her stretched out on a lounger. I was just about to put a call in to the director of ASA when I saw the Hispanic minder coming down the hillside. He was bare chested, and snapping pictures of Topaz as he approached. I stood and took aim with my tranquilizer rifle—waiting as he drew closer. But he stopped and, from a hidden sheath in back of him, produced a machete. I fired and hit him smack in the chest. He yelled, fell to his knees, and collapsed. Topaz sat up and screamed. I made my way to her, still with my rifle, like some suburban Great White Hunter. After calming her down, and calling O'Connell, I told her the story.

A police van soon arrived and they hauled off the assailant, who was just then coming around, mumbling in Spanish. O'Connell checked off a few items on a clipboard, wrote down my PI number, then winked and nudged me before he left.

Topaz was feeling better after finishing off my flask. She sent a nervous-looking Ivan off to buy a case of Bombay Sapphire gin.

Now we'll do some serious drinking, I was thinking. And...

"Now, Danny boy," Topaz purred, placing a hand on my arm. "About that bonus."

That night was an orgy of drinking and delightful perversion. When I woke up in the wee hours, I found Topaz in a deep sleep. I heard something outside and went to the window. There below, in a semi-secluded area, was a sight that I couldn't believe: on the exercise mat was Ivan the butler riding Marty Hoffman. Marty's teeth were bared and Ivan's expression shifted between maniacal and moronic. They moved off behind some bushes and I went back to bed.

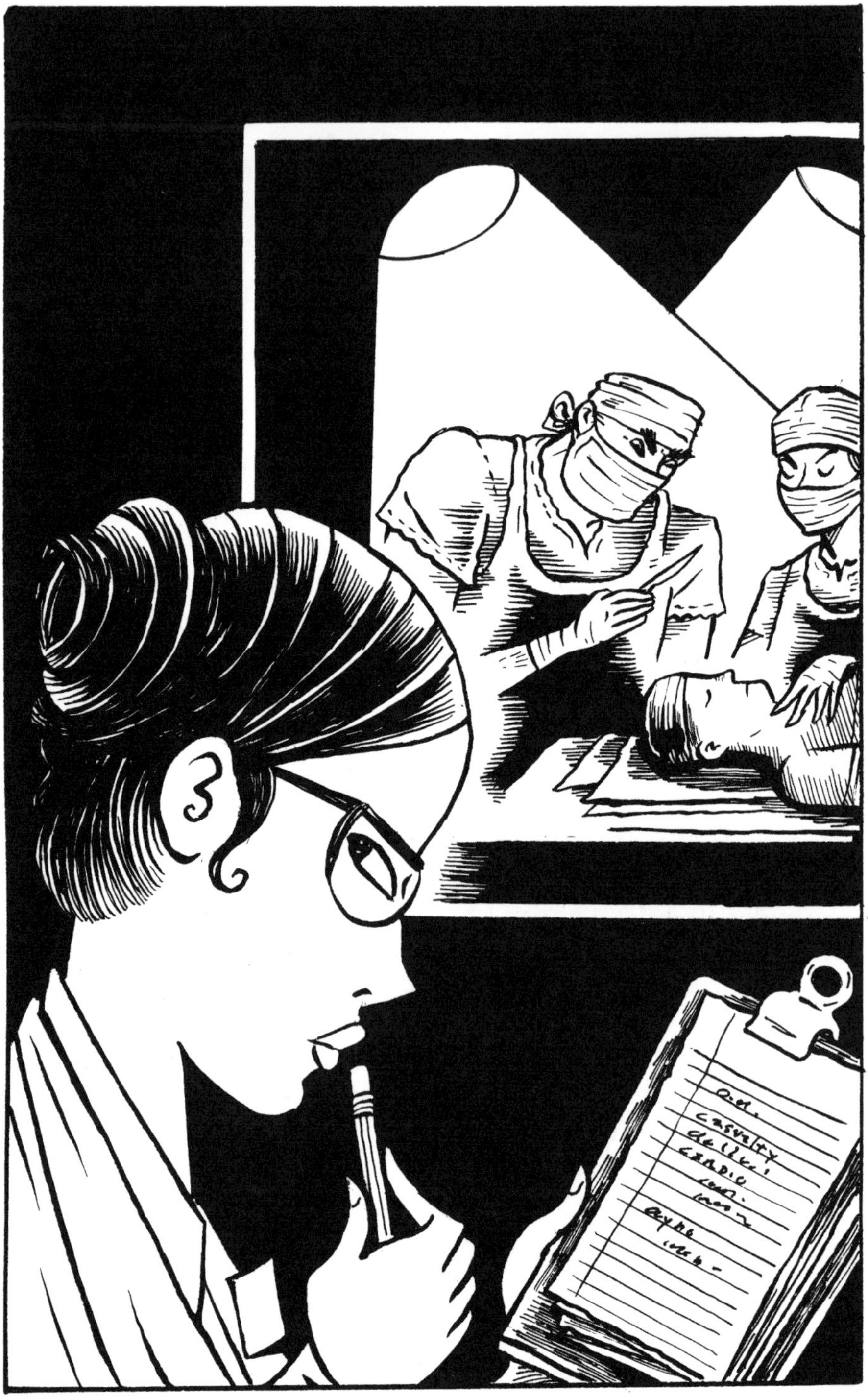

Jimmy Ballard's Hospital Review

Jimmy Ballard got out of the taxi and stood admiring the vast, impersonal buildings of the hospital whose wards and departments constituted a city unto itself. His mind was filled with the wonders of transplant surgery, the various highs induced by the deadpan team of anesthesiologists, and the haunted pictures displayed in the X-ray rooms. He had always suspected that this hospital was also part of an advanced psychological experiment. And now he was part of it. He was here to write the annual review for the Board.

On his first day the bookish yet sexually charged PR rep, Kate North, R.N., took him on a quick tour of the inpatient units, the operating theaters, the laundry, the kitchen, and finally the pharmacy/lab, where under a harsh light, a young West Indian wearing a lab coat focused on a small container of dark liquid. Kate North ignored him and he did not acknowledge their presence either. Even so, Ballard felt that there was some romantic bond between his guide and this intense pharmacist. As though reading Ballard's mind, Kate North quickly guided him along another busy hallway, holding his arm now as though he was a patient who had wandered away from his

A Loud Humming Sound Came From Above

assigned ward.

From a top tier of the main building, through a glass wall, they looked over the layout of the hospital. Ballard imagined the mental landscapes of the victims of road crashes, the pregnant women, the cancer patients, the kitchen staff preparing massive amounts of food, as well as the army in charge of linen for the 500 beds that were usually occupied. Kate North pointed out a staff lounge in a far corner that boasted an indoor courtyard with shrubs, trees, and an ornamental pool. A round skylight gave the pool and surrounding area a dose of natural light and a false feeling of open air and space. Ballard found this lounge the most unsettling of all the areas he would visit during his inspection.

The hospital was divided into three main sections: the central area housed primary clinical and emergency services, operating theaters, intensive care units, and maternity services. Around the central core were the psychiatric units, outpatient clinics, and administration offices. Grouped in the back were the service areas that provided the hospital with food and other supplies. Kate North pointed out the Accident and Emergency entrance, located near a hallway of shops and cafés. Had the architect thought that the emergency patients on entry might catch a glimpse of the diversions the hospital offered—as a kind of prize to motivate recovery?

Kate North escorted Ballard to his temporary office. "Tomorrow we'll visit the Casualty Department," she said flatly. Ballard watched her turn and walk away. He admired her athletic legs and the movement

Jimmy Ballard's Hospital Review

of her well-formed buttocks encased in a uniform that seemed a little tight for regulations; even a hint of black silk could be seen at the hem.

The Casualty Department

Kate's breath smelled of coffee and cigarettes, and mixed enticingly with the fumes of the Dior perfume she had dabbed on in the wee hours. In the staff area, she pulled Ballard aside so they could view the main reception room without being noticed. A man in greasy coveralls sat holding his crushed arm, with a drained look on his pockmarked face. A fat, red-faced man next to him held a swab of gauze over his eye and looked to be staring into space with the other one. Kate guided Ballard into a dark room where he half-expected her to unzip him, but instead she switched on a dim light and they stood looking through a one-way mirror into a small operating room. A doctor and nurse in scrubs were attending to a patient. A saline drip dangled from above and was inserted into the patient's arm. A nasty wound on his knee was exposed. The blood was sponged away by the nurse who then applied an antiseptic. The wound was finally sutured by the doctor, then wrapped in a dressing by the nurse.

"There are no new crash or burn injuries today," Kate said blandly, yet Ballard sensed a touch of chaos in her big, gray eyes. They exited the room and moved on to the blood bank, and Kate inquired at the reception desk as to when the next transfusion was scheduled, as if inquiring the next showing of a film at the local cinema. They watched the rather boring

A Loud Humming Sound Came From Above

procedure for a few minutes before she nudged him and they left.

Ahead, ambulance lights played off the corridor walls as Kate and Ballard made their way past the X-ray techs who slumped slightly, perhaps imitating their patients, weighed down by lead aprons. A couple of them stood sipping teas in their doorways, forlornly guarding their domain of equipment, darkrooms, and radiation residue.

Kate stopped and introduced Ballard to Dr. Stuart, head radiologist and diagnostic expert. Dr. Stuart wore black frame-glasses and a neatly trimmed mustache. His bluish-black hair gleamed under the fluorescent lights from ample application of hair gel. He reminded Ballard of a barber more than a doctor, and he seemed to be sizing up Ballard as well. Stuart invited them into his office and led them to seats that looked borrowed from a spacecraft. Stuart sat opposite, behind a wide blue steel desk. The color photos on the walls were all of children; Ballard was soon to learn they'd been photographed in Peru, where the doctor had done field work in his younger days. After a well-practiced recital of the hospital's features and the general functions of most departments, he began an in-depth discussion of his specialty. Here his passion poured forth and Ballard felt he was listening to an opinionated visual artist rather than a radiologist. Dr. Stuart segued into the proper preparation of a barium meal, as though he were a profiled chef working for a swank restaurant, determined to maintain its high rating in the Zagat Guide. Again, Kate seemed entranced as he spoke, and Ballard wondered if she'd had liaisons with all

Jimmy Ballard's Hospital Review

the prominent men at the hospital.

Ballard's mind wandered as they left Dr. Stuart. Had one too many documentaries been filmed in these corridors and departments, making his assignment redundant, even meaningless? How could his review ever compete with the cine-cameras, zoom lenses, and continuity people viewing the latest drama in the Trauma Ward? Ballard could imagine Dr. Stuart checking his makeup before stepping onto the set to explain the X-ray results to the frantic and distressed family members. The Board need only view these films to see that their experiment had taken on a life of its own.

Kate invited Ballard to lunch with some of her friends. "They're all techies," she said. "So you'll get a flavor of all their points of view." They chose a pizza parlor a short walk from the hospital and Ballard was the only male present. Holly, the stylish, brunette X-ray tech who wore her makeup so pale it approached that of a Goth rocker, worked exclusively with radiation treatment. She was the quiet one of the bunch, but occasionally exuded a sultry look between sips of Diet Coke and rearranging her salad on a paper plate. Betty, a middle-aged redhead with bottle-green eyes and a thin upper lip, called herself a mechanic and began describing in loving detail the various hospital equipment and machinery she worked on. Her discussion of a new type of laser might have continued for the entire lunch, had Kate not butted back in. The lab tech, Sharon, an Amazon who could have pursued a career as a fashion model but seemed ignorant of her especially good looks, wore little makeup and her

A Loud Humming Sound Came From Above

hair was cut into a messy style that she occasionally brushed out of her eyes. She talked about her duties with a curious zeal. Was she eager for a glowing report from him? Ballard wondered. He enjoyed listening to her while the others seemed to be daydreaming or scanning the room for potential lovers.

"I move from department to department," Sharon continued, touching Ballard's hand in a familiar way, "but, mostly, you'll find me in pathology. I'm the queen of the biopsies and the microtome. I study blood as well, some biochemistry, but lately it's been more work than I can handle from the doctors in microbiology. Bacteria today are becoming increasingly immune to the antibiotics at an alarming rate. And everybody is afraid of a pandemic." This brought everyone back and Kate looked especially disturbed.

Sharon laughed and said, "Don't worry. I'll always have a stash of antidotes for my friends." Everyone laughed but Ballard.

"She's joking, James," Betty said, winking like a drunken sailor.

"Is it true," Ballard asked, "that all gated communities in this district have medical tele-linkage with the hospital?" Kate answered in the affirmative and the others nodded silently.

On the walk back, Kate told him that there was a fifth member of their usual lunch group, Will Sanders, who was a physical measurement technician, but that he was out sick with the flu. His specialty was audiology; he suffered from hearing loss himself but wore an advanced aid not yet on the market that gave him the acute hearing abilities of a barn owl. In fact,

Jimmy Ballard's Hospital Review

he was nicknamed "The Fox," and his ears twitched when he tried to listen to anything a bit out of his range.

The Operating Theater

The surgical team entered the theater and approached the patient on the operating table. Each began their respective tasks. The nurse adjusted the patient's gown to expose the abdomen. She cleaned the skin with an antiseptic, then the surgeon outlined the area where the incision would be made. The anesthesiologist placed a mask over the face of the already unconscious patient.

Standing for a moment in the pose of a matador, the surgeon stepped forward and made his incision. One of the two assistant surgeons carefully swabbed the blood. In rapid succession, the surgeon cut through the layers of muscle. The anesthesiologist studied his instrument panel, making sure the patient was getting the right mixtures of gases. Both assistants clamped off the severed blood vessels and used retractors to pull back the skin and muscle flaps. The surgeon found the appendix and quickly removed it. The assistants worked together to remove the clamps and expertly sew up the incision. The surgeon bowed slightly to his team and departed. Ballard looked at his watch and saw that the whole process had taken under fifteen minutes. He thought of the faceless patient waking up later, groggy and sore and pressing the call button for a shot of morphine. He looked at his notes and the peculiar configuration of his drawing: surgeon,

A Loud Humming Sound Came From Above

anesthetic machine, assistants, nurse, operating light, patient, diathermy machine, and the instrument trolly that held the various surgical instruments: the dissecting forceps, operating scissors, and the scalpels.

"Tomorrow you'll have a day on your own," Kate said, escorting him back to his office. "Will you miss me?" she teased, making him smile and say yes. "But then Wednesday first thing. I'll be introducing you to all the big shots."

"Till then," Ballard said, taking Kate's hand and feeling the warmth of her palm, but instead of the look of seduction he was hoping for, her expression had shifted to business-as-usual. But she did finally throw him a vampy smile before heading off. Kate North was a mystery that he longed to solve.

The Hospital Doctors

When Kate and Ballard entered Dr. Kaminsky's office, led by his haughty secretary, they could see him across the room in a white lab coat, standing, viewing a computer screen, wearing headphones. His modish haircut came over the collar of his coat. He was writing something in a notebook. The secretary gestured toward two chairs that faced the doctor's desk and they sat down. Dr. Kaminsky finished up, removed his headphones, and turned to greet them. He was a young man, with generally good looks and a pleasant smile. Ballard stood briefly and shook hands with him.

"Excuse me, Mr. Ballard, but I prefer to stand

whenever I can." Dr. Kaminsky walked behind his desk, folded his arms, and cradled his chin with his right hand. "I'm an anesthesiologist, and so a key member of the surgical team. I, also, hold the patient's life in my hands." The doctor looked briefly at his hands. "We deliver the patient into the world of dreams, across the rivers of myth, to a multitude of netherworlds." He smiled beatifically. "The afterlife is previewed and it's nothing like what religions tell us. No, it's more like the mind of Dali or the hallucinations of the Huichol Indians of Northern Mexico." Dr. Kaminsky was charming and eloquent and peculiar. Ballard listened with interest as he keenly described his gases and drugs. He was also a contact if needed, set into position a year ago by the Board.

They moved on to Dr. Huber, a cardiologist, who was the opposite of the young Kaminsky, an older man with an annoyed presence, wearing a suit that would have better served a lawyer. He announced that his specialty, heart disease, was bound to affect everyone eventually. Dr. Huber touched his stethoscope and looked expectantly at Ballard, as if waiting for him to volunteer himself for a listen.

"My friends are the diagnostic machines in D Ward," he said with the wicked, impersonal smile of a new breed of gangster scientist. "They display for me the electrical patterns that help me to see certain blood vessels."

Next, Dr. Paul, the head pediatrician, was a tall, bony man in his early forties. He, too, wore a modish cut like Dr. Kaminsky, but Dr. Paul had a receding hairline, a Roman nose, and dull, brown eyes. He

A Loud Humming Sound Came From Above

wore a lab coat with lollipops, candy sticks, pens, and thermometers stuffed in the upper pocket. They met him in the hallway and as he talked he glanced around, monitoring the foot traffic in and out of his department. As they chatted, Ballard got the impression that Dr. Paul was covertly still a child himself, and a devious one at that—overly cautious about what he had to say. Even his expressions seemed borrowed from his adolescent patients. A smiling Eurasian nurse appeared with a young Down syndrome girl in tow. Dr. Paul abandoned their conversation and crouched to face his young patient. They communicated in some barely audible, secret language.

"This is Sybil, my star patient," he said, looking up at Ballard and Kate. Dr. Paul's entire face had transformed into a bright smile.

Sybil seemed only marginally affected by the Down syndrome and, after a quick study of the couple, offered her hand. Dr. Paul, Sybil, and the nurse moved on toward the hospital gift shop. Dr. Paul called back that they were going shopping, promising to meet up later in the Children's Ward.

Dr. Craig, the head gynecologist, appeared more like a strange policeman or some new type of security agent in his tight, powder blue uniform and Egyptian ankh bolo tie. How did this correspond to his arduous work in the domain of the vulva, pubis, labia, and reproductive system, Ballard wondered. But Dr. Craig cut the meeting short after taking a phone call—a call that Ballard suspected had been pre-arranged. As he walked away, Ballard noticed the many keys that swung from his belt, and a pair of rubber gloves that dangled from his back pocket. He appeared more like a sexual deviant posing as a doctor, Ballard decided. Kate stirred him from his thoughts, touching his lower back. Ballard imagined her as an ardent masseuse or chiropractor assessing the area she soon would be working on.

    The head pathologist, Dr. Rollins, an elderly man, they caught snoozing at his desk. Kate knocked loud enough on the open door to rouse him. He reminded Ballard of the French bulldog he had petted in the hospital parking lot the previous afternoon. Dr. Rollins's desk was piled with files and papers and books. Vials of what looked like blackish blood were haphazardly lying amongst a cigar, a thick men's spy-adventure paperback, and an open box of prophylactics. Dr. Rollins put his fingers together in a steeple and recited, in a monotone, his trials and tribulations as head pathologist. Kate soon appeared drowsy listening to the words that, clearly, made little sense to either of them.

    In the next office, the head psychiatrist insisted that Ballard call her Dorothy. But once they'd left their meeting with her, he had trouble recalling what she looked like, let alone what she had said. Ballard felt as though they had participated in some kind of brainwashing or hypnosis session. This crafty shrink would get a special note in his report.

    The last stop for the day was the office of the head surgeon, Dr. Spencer, whom they had watched perform the appendectomy. A hum leaked from some invisible machine in his office and Ballard noted that, like some mad maestro, he did not shake hands but

A Loud Humming Sound Came From Above

instead gave a slight bow. He reminded Ballard of a stage performer as he spoke and moved around his office, almost as though he were practicing steps and poses. Then he stood still, appearing again for a moment like a slightly unhinged matador. For such a large office, it was surprisingly bare, as if to emulate the surgery theater itself: his desk and bookcases were as sterile and empty as his operating tables. They said goodbye to Dr. Spencer and left him to his elaborate rehearsals.

"Do you have a little energy left for a visit to the Maternity Ward?" asked Kate.

"Of course, sure," Ballard said as she studied him over her glasses. He could see thickly applied black eyeliner and was lost for a moment in her beguiling eyes. Again she guided him by the arm, now as though he were a reluctant father trying to put off the inevitable obligation of facing his new offspring. He expected to hear babies crying, but the Maternity Ward was strangely silent, and Kate seemed to be enjoying his mystification. She pulled a white lab coat out of a supply closet and offered to help him on with it.

"It's better that you look like a doctor on this ward," she said, admiring the fit. In the first room, a midwife was checking a patient's rate of contractions. The patient smiled at them in a daze. Through a number of doors, they stepped into another room where a young mother was breastfeeding her infant. The bedcover was pulled back and her legs were bare. Kate seemed to bristle, perhaps suspecting that he was admiring the woman's legs.

Jimmy Ballard's Hospital Review

"There are supposed to be two, maybe even three, births later today, if you're interested," she said as she guided him along a window where the incubated babies were lying in clear, square compartments like some bad science fiction film.

He stopped to view a black baby who appeared almost purple in the gaudy lighting and the circulating swirls of purified air.

"Would you like to visit the Children's Ward? Dr. Paul and Sybil are probably there now."

Although Ballard was tired, he felt a boost as they entered the Children's Ward. The walls were painted in lively colors—one in glitzy red and yellow stripes that reminded him of a carnival tent. The beds were arranged in a circle and two laundry baskets were stuffed with toys. But the beds were empty, as though an abduction had just taken place. A stuffed bear and stuffed giraffe sat there, looking at them dumbly. The Eurasian nurse, Lee, came into the room and explained that the children had gone to the hospital garden. Lee had changed to a lab coat decorated with clowns, balloons, flowers, and butterflies. She led them to the window and they looked down at the line of children being led by Dr. Paul, the adult Peter Pan, and Sybil, an awkward Tinkerbell.

"Beyond the garden, they'll climb a summit and look back to view the hospital grounds in its entirety," Lee said, making a motion as though adjusting a troublesome corset.

Ballard spent the next day typing up his notes on an electric typewriter. At lunchtime, Kate tapped on his door in a playful mood.

A Loud Humming Sound Came From Above

"You know, James, you haven't asked me much about myself, or the nursing profession, for that matter."

"I'm sorry, Kate, it's a very general report."

"Aren't you interested in me?"

"Why, of course."

"Then take me to lunch?"

"Well, with pleasure."

"Good," said Kate with a coquettish look. "I've found a little bistro not too far. And no one has discovered it yet."

They left the hospital, boarded the Tube, and got off one station later. The restaurant was on the second level of a shopping complex: dark, comfy, something like a gentlemen's club. They settled themselves into a leather booth in one corner. They both ordered the crab stew special, and Ballard was pleased to see a good French wine on the menu. During lunch, Kate spoke of growing up in London, her early disillusionment with art school, the great thrill of the early punk scene, and a summer of bumming around the beaches of Greece and Turkey. After a profound dream where she'd been a nurse on a battlefield, she became obsessed with the profession. For once, her parents gave her their complete support and even paid for nursing school. From the beginning, she had studied hard. After graduation, she'd worked in many of the different specialties: intensive care, psychiatry, midwifery, elder care, pediatrics, but finally found her true calling in public relations.

"But what was the most challenging before you took this job?" Ballard asked, and wondered just what had so attracted him to this independent young lady twenty-three years younger than he was.

"The elderly," she said, looking at him as though he had somehow just been transformed into Herbert Humbert, and she into a more sophisticated Lolita. "And it was also the most rewarding." She sipped her wine and stared off across the empty room, perhaps picturing some stressful life-changing experience she'd had while working in the world of geriatrics.

"Depression is widespread with this age group," she said. "But I worked under a brilliant doctor who knew the cure and used it: opiates. During that time, the ward for the elderly was an even happier place than the Children's Ward. He determined the dose each patient could tolerate while remaining functional and then prescribed that dose as needed. Pain complaints ceased almost completely. He also supplied other drugs if the patient had a preference; cannabis extract was very popular.

"During this period, one patient, who'd been a notorious swinger in the Sixties, filled notebooks with her racy memoirs that were later published. And a fantastic art show was exhibited by the elderly patients; it was reviewed by the local media and even caused a bit of controversy. A certain eighty-seven year-old, Mr. Simon Thurston, had obtained Polaroids of his disfigured penis from his medical files and displayed them as found art.

"There were a few musicians there at that time who held impromptu concerts. They covered Stravinsky, mariachi music, and even some cool jazz. They changed the lighting in the ward to a mix

A Loud Humming Sound Came From Above

of soft golden splashes and dreamy purple shades, which helped to transform it into an atmosphere of a decadent nightclub-cum-opium-den. But it couldn't last, of course. The doctor was exposed and booted from the hospital.

"I secretly agreed with his treatment," she added quietly, as though someone might be listening. "But soon after the scandal, things went back to their old gloomy ways, and after some night classes, I applied for a position in public relations." Ballard made a mental note of the doctor's name to file a petition to have him reinstated.

The following day, Kate introduced him to a blur of people. She seemed to take some pleasure in making the endless introductions, including the staff from the hospital gift shop; the manager of the on-site radio station; the chaplain again, whom Ballard managed to neatly brush off; and a sexy, young couple that he was surprised and delighted to find were the hospital disc jockey and beautician.

The Hospital at Night

The first thing Ballard noticed was the absence of activity in the hallways. The quietude was enhanced by dim lighting throughout the corridors and waiting rooms. He stopped by a room where a red light above the door was flashing. At the far end of the hallway, Dr. Huber and two nurses were hurrying towards him. Dr. Huber urged Ballard inside. In a moment, they were all in the patient's room.

In bed was an elderly woman lying on the covers,

motionless. Her head was to the side and an arm was dangling over the bedside. A night nurse explained to Dr. Huber that heart massage and mouth-to-mouth resuscitation had both failed. Dr. Huber watched his team set up two trolleys of machines, including a defibrillator. An oxygen mask was strapped onto her by one nurse and a tube was guided down her throat. The electrocardiogram equipment was set in place and Dr. Huber studied the readout and then placed the shock pads on the patient's chest. After two jolts, the woman was revived. She sat up with an almost serene expression and the team quietly congratulated her.

"Send Mrs. Martin to IC for a few days," Dr. Huber instructed the night nurse. He turned to Ballard with a nod and then he was gone. Ballard walked out of the room and down another hallway, letting some inner sense of navigation guide him. He wandered the back corridors and looked into the empty rooms and offices. He came across a few porters in a waiting room watching news on TV and drinking tea. He continued on his inspection and spoke with a few women from domestic services. The kitchen was open so he bought a coffee and headed to his office.

Medical Engineering

The clear plastic-covered booklet on his desk, probably left by Kate North since she knew his interest in this field, was titled: Medical Engineering, 1984. The cover diagram depicted a green, human form showing all the current spare parts of the human body in yellow, with corresponding numbers. One leg and arm

A Loud Humming Sound Came From Above

were orange and obviously artificial. The illustration could have doubled for the cover of a deranged science fiction collection. He read the listing slowly.

1. **Wig.**
2. **Skull plate.**
3. **Skull plug.**
4. **Plastic cornea.**
5. **Plastic eye.**
6. **Contact lenses.**
7. **Spectacles.**
8. **Hearing aid.**
9. **False teeth.**
10. **Chin enlarger.**
11. **Artificial larynx.**
12. **Pacemaker.**
13. **Artificial breast.**
14. **Shoulder joint.**
15. **Artificial arm.**
16. **Synthetic artery.**
17. **Heart valves.**
18. **Elbow joint.**
19. **Synthetic vein.**
20. **Elbow cap.**
21. **Elbow hinge.**
22. **Abdominal patch.**
23. **Hip joint.**
24. **Testicle implants.**
25. **Artificial knee.**
26. **Femur.**
27. **Finger joints.**
28. **Knee joints.**

Jimmy Ballard's Hospital Review

29. Knee plate.
30. Shinbone.

Ballard turned the page and the next fantastic drawing was of an artificial hand with its "Arm socket, motor with amplifier and gears," and its "Rechargeable battery pack." Another page showed an X-ray, perhaps taken by one of Dr. Stuart's assistants. The finger joints of stainless steel were already in position in a skeletal hand. Another page displayed the devilish and confusing diagram of a heart-lung machine. Below it was a pacemaker, looking something like a lighter except for the plastic tubing that was attached to it.

He worked on his review throughout the day, breaking only for brief meetings with a physiotherapist and a psychotherapist who had both just returned from holidays in Spain. Afterward, he found himself near the hospital pharmacy/lab. This time, the West Indian pharmacist wished him a cheery good afternoon.

Ballard made brief visits over the next few days to the more mundane outpatient department, admissions office, medical records, the hospital switchboard, and the supplies department. On his final rounds, he looked for Kate North in the staff lounge where he instead spotted Dr. Rollins, coming out of a back room with Lee, the Eurasian nurse from the Children's Ward. Rollins shot him a quick, contemptuous look, then tried to smile. Lee looked away but he thought he'd glimpsed a slightly bruised lip.

In the cafeteria, Ballard asked Betty and Sharon where Kate might be. Sharon grinned and sent him

A Loud Humming Sound Came From Above

on what turned out to be a wild goose chase. During his last days, Kate was never where she was supposed to be. He was starting to suspect a conspiracy. Eventually, he stood by her office for nearly an hour, looking periodically at a small notebook before, finally feeling foolish, deciding to give up.

Ballard knew that compiling the psychology of the future was the ultimate aim. The Board would be pleased to see that the inner migration continued unabated. There would always be the variants, the Dr. Craigs and the Dr. Rollinses. But as they were the first of the inevitable deviant behaviors that would erupt from time to time, they, too, would be studied and contained. Dr. Craig would have to go, of course, before he plotted some kind of insane takeover. Ballard had photographed the documents in his files that indicated this tendency. So far, Craig and Rollins had interfered only slightly with the psychic fulfillment that otherwise looked to be flourishing since the Board had put its systems into place. And there were a few others who needed further monitoring, but so far, showed no major glitches.

Ballard finished typing his report and placed the sheaf of papers in a white plastic case. He would present it to the Review Board the following week. On this, his last day, he had hoped to invite Kate to his favorite restaurant in Chelsea, but wondered again if she'd been avoiding him.

He left the hospital, left the grounds, and headed off down a busy city street. It started to rain heavily and he had not brought an umbrella.

He hurried along, looking through the blur of

rain for a place to duck into. Shielding his face with the briefcase, he spotted the restaurant where he had eaten with Kate. An exquisite girl, decked out in an open black slicker and stiletto heels, stood under the awning at the entranceway, making him think of a Helmut Newton photograph.

Kate North smiled at him as he approached, now dripping wet. For the first time, she was wearing her hair down and no glasses. She wiped off his face and kissed his mouth, biting at his lip.

"I was just looking for you inside," she whispered into his ear.

"Now, the real review will begin," Ballard said, realizing his voice had dropped to a lower register.

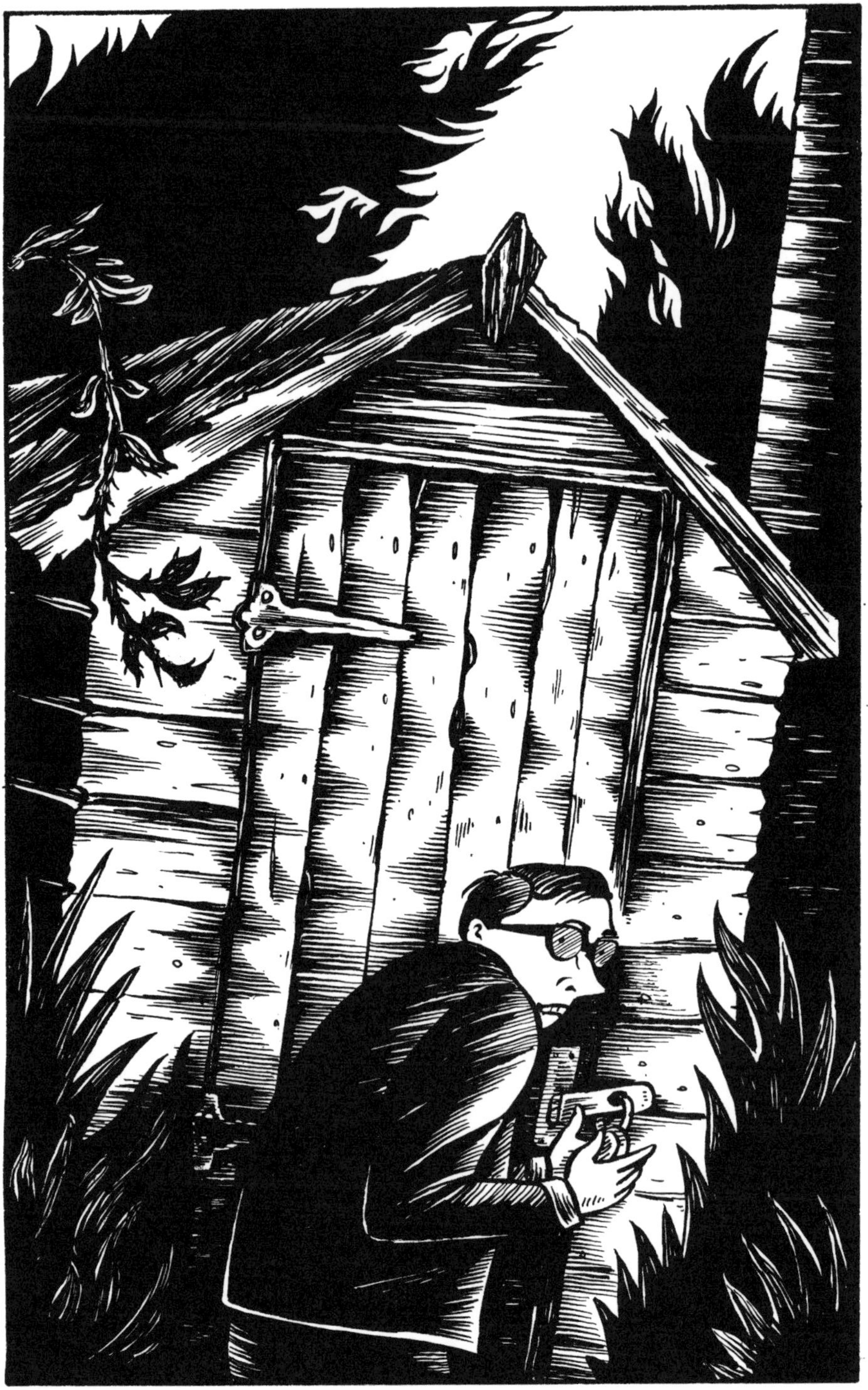

CRAZY CARL'S THING

7:45 A.M. My first intake at the methadone clinic. "Raven" was a twenty-five-year-old stripper. She spilled some coffee on my desk, giggled, and made a half-hearted attempt to wipe it up with her sleeve. Her right eye was swollen and I thought she'd been slugged.

"No," she said, "I tried to hit a vein in my neck. But I was drunk."

Raven wiped her runny nose with the other sleeve. "I thought maybe I'd hit an artery because I went into a seizure. This morning, my eye was all swollen and shit."

"Are you working?" I asked. She said yes, no, that some money was owed, and then added huffily, "I can work whenever I want."

For something to do besides the mundane paperwork, I decided to ask these incoming clients what the most exciting thing was they'd ever done.

I asked Raven and she said, "Oh, I dunno."

8:30 A.M. Thirty-three-year-old homeless man who stank: something like compost and rotting rubber sandals. I directed my fan at him.

"What's the most exciting thing you've ever done?" I asked, trying not to breathe through my nose.

A Loud Humming Sound Came From Above

"When I went to Tucson with my dad," he said. "I'd just turned fourteen. My life's been pretty boring."

After he left, I sprayed the chair with Medi-Aire, a "biological odor eliminator."

Bryan stuck his head into my office and said he'd do Dark City Man's intake. I took a look in the waiting room: long black coat, black hat something like a bowler, shaved head, pale as chalk, definitely reminiscent of the aliens in the film.

My office was saturated with the soapy smelling Medi-Aire.

Bryan sniffed. "Had a ripe one, eh?"

9:17 A.M. Fifty-year-old man called "Jacko."

Most exciting thing?

"That had to have been the time I parachuted from a plane at twenty-five-hundred feet. I was a bartender then. My boss was always getting us together for some damn fool thing."

Forty-five-year-old homeless man who looked twenty years older. His premature aging was due a lot to lifestyle: poor diet, lack of medical attention, and so forth.

Most exciting?

"Probably when I was in the Navy. I was on a submarine crew in Hawaii. One time, we surfaced and a whole group of dolphins appeared and started leaping over the sub. That was pretty exciting."

9:53 A.M. thirty-six-year-old man who, in spite of his Wild West mustache, looked his age—maybe even younger. Nickname: "Slim."

Exciting?

"What, like fucking a supermodel or some-

Crazy Carl's Thing

thing?"

"Okay," I said. "Did you?"

"No. I went with a few dancers, though. But that was a long time ago."

During the intake, I could see that Slim was still thinking it over. "What, like winning the lotto or something?"

12:15 P.M. Sixty-eight-year-old ex-con. Ex-biker. Moniker: "Hog."

Most exciting?

"Oh, I guess when I went to Germany. I went to this huge castle out there in the Black Forest. I had to walk for miles to get to it, but it was worth it. There was a moat, catapults, even some wild boar."

Fifty-two-year-old man who bore an uncanny resemblance to Shakespeare.

Exciting?

"Two sexual encounters," said William. "There was one fine lady who made love to me. She got on top and rubbed her breasts right in my face. The other, a nymphet, began the lovemaking by sucking on my toes. I'll never forget either of them."

Fifty-one-year-old computer programmer, "Nick," screwed up his face and gave the question some thought.

He laughed. "Oh, maybe the first time I tried heroin." Later he came back to my office to say, "No, I believe it was the time I did some acrobatic flying with my brother. But that was twenty-some years ago."

1:03 P.M. twenty-three-year-old homeless man who told me he camped by a phone booth and used that number as his own. I told him about a family

A Loud Humming Sound Came From Above

in Morocco who lived in a wrecked car and used the license plate as their mailing address.

Most exciting?

"I fired off a .50 caliber BMG machine gun out in the desert once."

1:23 P.M. Seventy-three-year-old ex-seaman. A ghostly character right out of Conrad, his arms were smeared black with crude tattoos.

"It had to have been the time I swam in the Mariana Trench," he said. "It's the deepest area of sea in the world."

2:10 P.M. Forty-four-year-old parolee. His dark, reptilian eyes scanned the room in a series of quick moves.

"People call me 'Slick'," he said, "cuz I'm always hitting licks."

Most exciting?

"Some people feel it was their crimes," I said to prompt him, and his eyes danced.

"Yeah," Slick agreed. "I've done lots of stuff, robberies—I shot a guy in the ass once," he snickered. "I love guns but I can't have 'em anymore. Once I was shanghaied by this nut who was gonna kill me, his old lady, and then probably himself. He had me driving her car. He was in the back with a shotgun. In the rear view mirror, I seen that he'd dropped his cigarette. I slammed the brakes and me and the bitch jumped him."

"He begged me not to kill him." Slick snorted. "Then the cunt comes back to my place for his fuckin' jacket. I had my gun and told him to get the fuck out. Then I shot him in the ass." Slick's smile contrasted

Crazy Carl's Thing

weirdly with his vacant stare.

2:15 P.M. My last intake of the day was a timid man with short, black hair, wearing red-tinted black-frame glasses. He was thirty-two and received an SSI check that was almost as much as I made working full-time. When I asked "Carl" the "most exciting thing" question, he asked if he could close the office door, which was just barely open.

After shutting the door, he sat back down and in a hushed voice, said, "I can't tell you. I'd have to show you. It's something I've recently acquired."

Although we were forbidden to fraternize with clients, I agreed to meet him at a café a few blocks away. When I arrived, Carl quickly steered me down the street, anxious to show me his "most exciting thing."

"It's not far," he said for the second time, on the fourth block of the walk. Finally, we stopped and he gestured to a weathered apartment building that sent a short, melancholy shiver over me. Around the back, we traveled a path through a mostly dirt yard. At the end was a concrete shed. When we got to the door, Carl turned to me. "I'll have to charge you two dollars."

"What?" I had come this far so I peeled off two George Washingtons. He opened the serious-looking padlock and then the door itself. He turned to me again.

"Please wait for just one moment. I'll be right back."

Could Carl be dangerous? There was something downright creepy going on.

A Loud Humming Sound Came From Above

When he returned, I insisted that I follow him in. Carl led the way with a small flashlight, even though the room could be made out from a dim light on the other side. Another, even dimmer, light shone from inside an old-style tent.

"Well, you've paid your money," he said. "You're entitled to your look."

He directed his flashlight beam at the opening of the tent.

With one eye on Carl and one on the tent, I approached the entrance, squatting down to completely pull back the flap. A stuffed two-headed calf greeted me. One head looked right, the other left, and the eyes were dark and sad and strange. The floor was covered with straw and there was even a bucket of water. Carl was staring at the floor as I took one last look at the freak of nature.

Outside, Carl smiled beatifically. "He's from God, you know," he said softly. "And he still has the power of God, even though he died."

"Sure, Carl." I thanked him and went on my way.

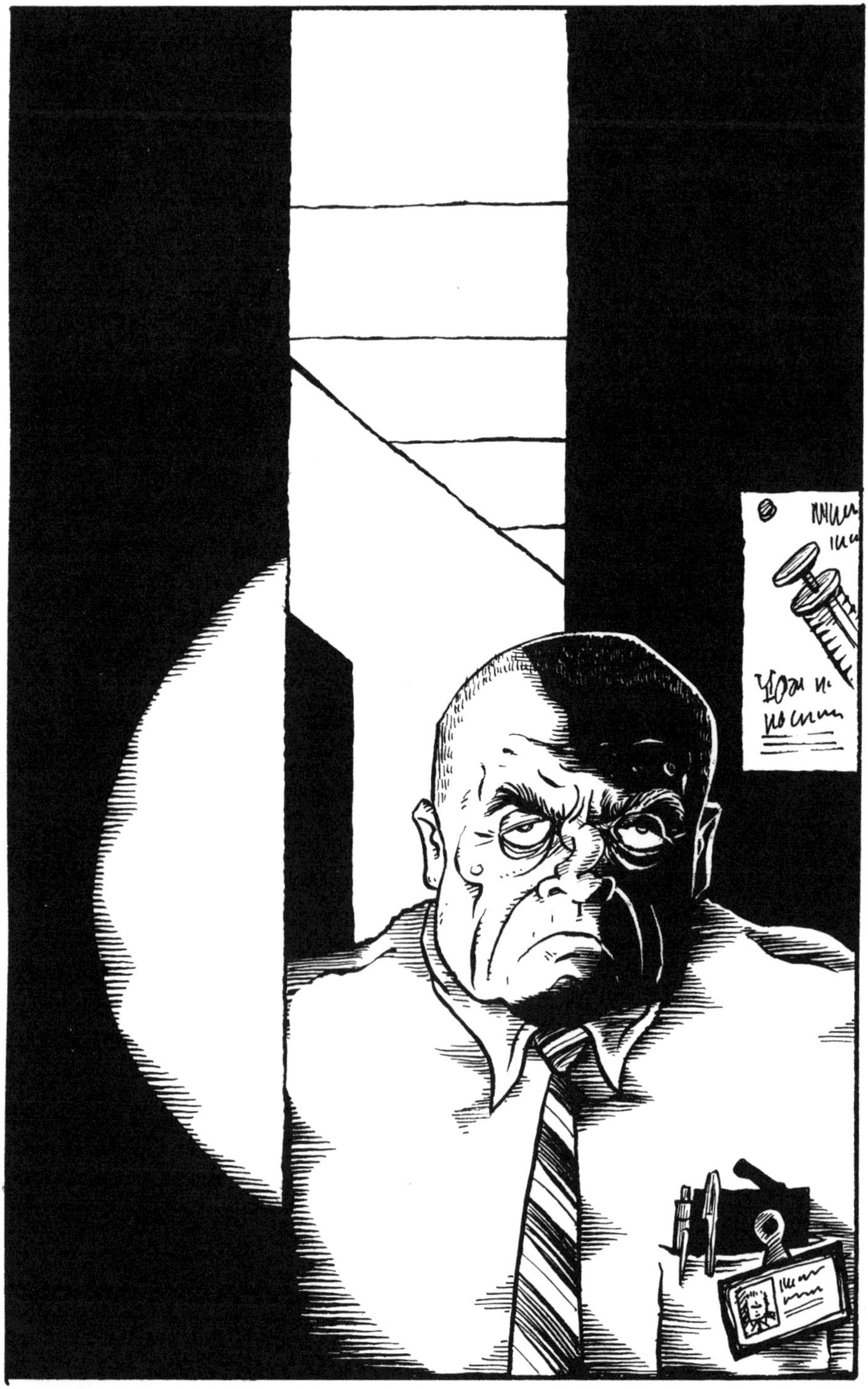

The Methadone Clinic

On a morning walk, I ran into a junkie couple. I knew the guy, a huge deathlike figure with bad teeth who always wore sunglasses; I didn't know the girl, but she was friendly, even took off her dark glasses at one point, showing me pinned eyes. She looked like she could use some dental work as well. We talked about Border Collies (since someone had passed by with one and we'd all stopped to admire and pet it), and the clinic and its eventual shutdown by the State. The junkie couple went on their way and I resumed my walk, thinking back some more about the old clinic days.

"The Clinic" was the methadone clinic where I'd once been a client, and then a detox counselor. Before I was a counselor, I was the "client rep"—a fairly meaningless title: I was given a small stipend to attend the weekly staff meetings, to poster the Tenderloin with ads for "treatment" the clinic offered, and to help with things like the Thanksgiving Day picnic. I remember well that first Thanksgiving picnic held in Golden Gate Park. Imagine a group of burned-out drug addicts, half of them pregnant women, sitting and nodding around a picnic table, their kids running rampant, and a couple of the adults finally falling face-forward into their plastic plates of turkey with all the trimmings.

I'd been on the twenty-one day detox program numerous times until I finally decided to go on maintenance and taper off over a year. I knew that a methadone dose, like a heroin habit itself, is what you got used to. I continued to taper and give clean urinalysis samples. I honestly didn't think much about using. I'd made the trade in my mind, and my desire to get high was mostly fulfilled with the glow I got from my daily dose. I also smoked pot, and drank now and then. A side effect of methadone was that you could imbibe without getting really bombed, and the next day's dose would magically clear the rare hangover. The counselors warned us about drinking, and made us take a Breathalyzer test on occasion; if our alcohol levels were too high, our dose was reduced by half or, in some cases, withheld completely. Thankfully, they didn't test for marijuana. It went nicely with the methadone high, too. When I'd been using dope, I'd never thought of smoking weed or drinking, but they both seemed to enhance the methadone glow.

So a year later, I "graduated" from the methadone program and took my last dose of three milligrams. I'd begun to experience typical withdrawal symptoms: low energy, hot flashes, diarrhea, headaches, sniffles, runny nose, what felt like aching bones, and an impossible, inner emptiness. But I was determined and, after a couple of weeks, I started to feel better. A few months later, I was back to normal. But I was broke, since my insurance checks had run out, so I took a job driving cab.

Almost a year later, I got a letter from the director

The Methadone Clinic

of the methadone clinic. They were having an alumni celebration for the clients who had graduated in the last couple of years. I was curious. The day of the event arrived and I showed up to find only the director. We laughed about it over coffee and cake and I got an idea: "How about hiring me as a counselor?" The director, an immigrant from Hungary who was a medical school dropout and an ex-user himself, gave it some thought. He asked me to write a proposal explaining why I thought I was qualified to work as a counselor. That night I typed out a couple of pages that got me the job.

There were two types of counseling at the clinic: detox and maintenance. Detox consisted of a 21-day tapering off program and was repeated by most users to the point where they became regulars. Undergoing maintenance, one could find a holding dose, which could continue for as long as a person showed up—sometimes a lifetime. But there were other factors: a "dirty" urine specimen would cause the dose to be raised; nonpayment for services would cause the dose to be lowered; and finally, the "approved clinic taper," allowed once a client had given three months of clean UAs and had paid up their fees.

As a detox counselor, I gave out the standard information, but word got around that I'd been successful, and so some clients began to seek me out for advice. Most seemed less than enthralled with my nonsense answers and straightforward approach: I'd stopped hanging out with people who used heroin, I'd dosed daily, and I'd stuck to my taper. I told them that, in retrospect, I was sure I could've

A Loud Humming Sound Came From Above

done the same thing on the twenty-one day detox and that if I had to do it over, that's exactly what I'd do. The withdrawal symptoms, once you get to them, are basically the same—the taper only postpones them. Once you get through the withdrawal, it's mostly a head game. An added annoyance is that methadone has a longer withdrawal timeframe than heroin. But I'd tell them, "If you think you need more than 21 days to be successful, then get on the maintenance program. If you prefer to do it quickly and move on, then make the detox work. It's up to you."

"Well what about support groups?" they'd ask. "NA? The Twelve Steps?"

I told them that all the war stories and the whining weren't for me. "But everybody's different," I said, "It might be just the ticket for you. I had a friend who went through it successfully, using Satan as his higher power." A lot of clients were astounded when I'd share my true feelings. "Do as thou wilt shall be the whole of the law," I'd quote old Aleister Crowley. They'd never heard this approach from a counselor.

Still, some clients persisted in their belief that I had some occult ingredient for success; they wanted to hang out and talk. This wasn't easy in detox, since it was a front-line, quick-moving process. But I made time for them later in the day, once the intakes and paperwork were done. I explored the possibility with them that there was an unconscious activity at work as well, something like what Colin Wilson had coined "Faculty X." Wilson believed Faculty X was in play during all psychic phenomena: a part of the brain that modern man had lost touch with. And perhaps this

152

The Methadone Clinic

Faculty X was activated in the person who'd finally decided not to turn back?

"Gimme my juice!" I remembered one irate black man yelling at a dosing nurse who was being difficult one day. Such little acts of rebellion are what stuck out most pleasantly in my memory. I remember another client, a stripper, who was being given a hard time by one of the intake workers I didn't like. Finally, the intake woman called the client's counselor who confirmed that, indeed, she was supposed to fork over her dosing card, because it was her final dose before permanently transferring to another clinic. Reluctantly, she gave up the card. After taking her dose, the stripper strode back over to the intake worker who continued to glare at her.

"Whataya looking at, pig face?" she said loud enough for everyone within earshot, then laughed crazily before leaving. I'd been watching, unseen, and went back to my office chuckling. Pig Face, stunned, immediately went around the clinic asking the other employees, "Did you hear what she called me?" She seemed to sense the awful triumph of the transferring client as she went back to her post. She had acquired a nickname that would be used regularly behind her back.

Black market methadone was another option to keep a sick user well. I'd bought it for home cures, which were mostly successful for varying amounts of time. Some clients with good records and clean UAs who had jobs were given "take-homes" in a little locked metal box. Some were given up to five plastic bottles (One hundred or more milligrams each) of

A Loud Humming Sound Came From Above

the pale red dope water with the stale cherry taste. And there was the disgusting practice of "mouthing it." Once outside the clinic, the client would spit their dose into an old bottle and sell it. The dosing nurses were supposed to make sure the clients spoke before they left the window, but they'd get busy and forget. Sometimes, people got held up for their boxes, and the police would come in and talk with the dosing nurses and director. Some of these "robberies" were set up by the clients themselves.

There was always a lot of drug dealing in the general vicinity of the clinic, an activity which I secretly supported since it added to the drama and color of the neighborhood. But the majority of the clinic staff was in a huff about it, trying to bust the dealers, whom I viewed as entrepreneurs of the street. Since dealing and "middling" between buyer and seller had been my only job until I'd begun driving cab, I sympathized with street dealers. I wondered if the staff's resentment was borne of competition, since the clinic was, in actuality, the biggest drug dealer in town. For the most part, I kept these ideas to myself, only sharing them with a few clients and the even fewer sympathetic staff members.

The neighborhood was grimy with the overspill of a homeless shelter, and lurid with neon signs for massage parlors, a porno shop, and an after-hours rave club. It was amusing in the mornings, seeing the flamboyantly dressed ravers coming out of the club as the "methadonians" lined up next door. The ravers, still high on X, were slightly appalled at the junkies at first. But they got used to them, and the clients were

The Methadone Clinic

entertained to no end by the lavishness of the ravers who were only then ending their night of partying. There was one man with bright orange, spiky hair, who wore a skintight suit of the same color. The next week, his hair would be lime-green and he'd be wearing a lime-green suit. One morning, an old client, resembling some lost and slightly mad prospector, pointed him out. "That there guy is my hero," he grinned.

Another morning, I stepped out front for some air and saw four Guardian Angels coming down the street. I stopped them and introduced myself; they viewed me skeptically. They'd just set up "headquarters" down the block and were out on their first patrol. Their demeanor and attitude reminded me of the droogs in *A Clockwork Orange*. But I told them about the clinic's newsletter and how I might write something about them, so they invited me to stop by their headquarters sometime. The following week, I decided to pay them a visit. I'd read their founder Curtis Sliwa's book, which offered some basic information on how to avoid being attacked or robbed on the streets. When I arrived, one of the Angels patted me down before I was allowed admittance to the apartment they'd rented. I noticed a tall stack of empty pizza cartons in the corner of the dirty kitchen. I got out my notebook and asked why they weren't in a more dangerous neighborhood. The one who looked to be in charge said that they showed up wherever they were requested, and the residents and shop owners in this particular neighborhood had requested them. To me, it looked as though they did a lot more pizza-eating than citizenry-protecting. I never wrote the article about them. After a while, they disappeared from the neighborhood.

The Hungarian clinic director was relocated to a less demanding job in the administration building, and the detox manager was fired at the same time. The clinic suddenly had a new director and a new manager of detox. The former detox manager was a quiet, frail woman who'd mostly stayed in her office and did very little. Detox pretty much ran itself, so she easily got away with it, until enough reports were lodged against her to make Admin take a look. They quickly found that she played a lot of computer poker and spent a lot of time in online chat rooms.

The new director and the detox manager were middle-aged men. I'd heard that Robert Gaines, the new detox manager, was going to be a problem, that he'd been handed a load of extra work with his new position, and that he'd distribute this workload to anyone who was under him: office workers, nurses, detox counselors, security, even the janitor. Word was out.

My turn came to report to Robert Gaines and there he sat at his desk, reading something on the computer screen. Gaines had a large head and flat ears. He wore a buzz cut as though recently released from the army or escaped from a cult. He looked like a dull brute, too—his eyes tired and stupid and crazed. Already I wanted to kill him.

After the phony formalities, he began, "Tom, I notice that the afternoons in detox are really slow." He emphasized the word *really*.

"Well, that's not really true," I countered. "That's when we catch up with our paperwork, and see other clients for follow-up appointments. And...um, there's

The Methadone Clinic

usually still some stragglers who sign up late."

"Well, I'd like you to do your paperwork during the intake process," he said, emphasizing *during*.

"Uh, well, we do write up the treatment plan with the client, but if we did our case notes, too, well...we wouldn't get the detoxes done in the morning. A lot of clients would have to come back after lunch."

"No, I don't want that. Can't you work faster?"

"Do you want to be able to read legible, concise, thoughtful notes or just some standard rushed-off nonsense?" I shot back.

Gaines was getting upset: his eyes became hard and his breathing became audible. He looked back at his screen.

"I need you and the other detox counselor to do different work in the afternoons," he said, his face showing a dangerous contortion of emotions as he looked back at me.

I decided to try and put into practice a new style of therapy I was studying called Rational Emotive Therapy. Among other things, RET helped one to keep destructive emotions in check by discovering one's "musts" and "absolute demands," and challenging them. I began doing this by telling myself that if Robert Gaines wanted to be disagreeable, he could: although I'd prefer that he wasn't.

"It'll be various duties," Gaines was saying, having regained his composure. "You'll learn about the work as it's assigned to you. And when you have any downtime, I want you both to report to me."

It was obvious my whole work environment and daily schedule was to turn into a hellish existence.

A Loud Humming Sound Came From Above

I looked at Gaines's smug expression. This was the reason I'd stayed away from legitimate work for so long. I decided then and there that I'd deal with it as it unfolded, rather than try and reason with him at that moment. I didn't say anything more, although Gaines looked ready for more confrontation. Finally he said, "Okay, that'll be all then, Tom. I'll be by tomorrow after lunch with some new work."

The following day, I purposely wrote my notes very slowly and made sure I had plenty to do in the afternoon. It turned out to be a heavy day of intakes as well, and the doctor allowed even more people to sign up after lunch. At 1:30 P.M. I shut my office door and hung the "Do Not Disturb" sign. I began to write up case notes for the fifteen intakes I'd done. Suddenly, the door swung open and there stood Robert Gaines with a stack of files up to his chin. He stepped in and dropped them on my desk on top of my spread out notes.

"Tom, I need to teach you how to do a 50-mile radius check on all of these patients."

"Honestly, Mr. Gaines, this isn't the day for anything new," I said hopelessly. "We had twenty-six intakes today." I gestured toward my notes and managed to pull some of them from under his pile of charts. "I have just enough time to finish up before closing."

Gaines's face became a Halloween grimace that was hard to look at. "I don't care!" His voice rose dangerously. "I need this work done now!"

Going over the RET quickly in my head, I thought: There's no law saying that he can't be irrational. I don't

The Methadone Clinic

rule the universe." Gaines was glaring at me, waiting for a response. I took a breath.

"Listen, Mr. Gaines, I have a job to do. Once that's done, I'll be glad to help you."

The new detox manager's enraged expression seemed frozen there before me. I looked down and resumed writing my notes. Gaines grabbed the charts knocking some of my papers to the floor, before plowing back through the door. I knew that he'd go to the new director to file a report. I instructed the receptionist to hold all my calls and take messages. I finished my work right at 3 P.M., punched out, and didn't run into anyone on my way out the less traveled back entrance.

The following morning, I punched in and got a chilly look from Robert Gaines, who ignored my pleasant good morning greeting when I passed him in the hallway. About midday, I received a phone call.

"Tom Giles?"

"Yes."

"Hi Tom, this is Nathan Caldwell, the new director."

"Hello, Mr. Caldwell. What can I do for you?"

"Do you have time to come upstairs and meet with me?"

Caldwell was not smiling when I entered his office, but we shook hands and he motioned me to a seat. He was a fiftyish, heavyset man who seemed comfortable and happy with that fact. On his desk were a briefcase, a large coffee, and a bag of donuts waiting to be devoured. I was sure that Caldwell, the devourer, wanted to give all of his attention to the

A Loud Humming Sound Came From Above

donuts ASAP, so I figured wrapping things up quickly would be a good move.

"I wish this was strictly an introductory meeting and I'm sure you do as well," I said. "But I believe I know why you wanted to see me."

Caldwell was cool. He didn't say anything, and allowed only the faintest smile to cross his lips.

"I've told Mr. Gaines that I'd be glad to help out with any other work, as long as my regular duties were completed. And yesterday was not the day for learning new work, with twenty-six intakes. He must have known this."

Caldwell peeled the lid off of his coffee and took a greedy sip.

"How do you propose that we solve this problem, Tom?"

On instinct, I stood and said, "Let me do my best to work out this situation without involving you. I'm sure you have more pressing issues to deal with today."

Caldwell seemed a little surprised, but then he looked relieved, and even thanked me. "Let's talk again, once things have calmed down," he said, standing and walking me to the door, ignoring his ringing phone.

I didn't really have any idea how to deal with Robert Gaines but I thought at least I'd bought some time. A few days went by and gradually Gaines began to communicate with me again.

"Tom, today I want Sharina to do all of the intakes so I can train you to do some other tasks."

He'd caught me off guard; I was getting ready

The Methadone Clinic

to do an intake, happy with myself for having evaded his wrath all week. I decided to continue my stand. It being Friday, I wouldn't have to see his face again until Tuesday, since Monday was a holiday.

"Mr. Gaines," I said. "I'm sorry but I have a lot of follow-ups today, a temporary transfer to arrange, and a stack of charts to close."

Gaines's expression, if not frightening, was certainly unnerving. "You must do what I say!" he commanded, drawing attention to us. "I could write you up for insubordination," he added in a lower tone. "I want you to postpone all your other work until next week."

"No-can-do," I said, going on automatic. "If I don't do this transfer, the client won't be able to dose in LA. And it's too late to change my follow-ups. If my charts aren't closed today they'll be out of compliance with the State. And the State is above you."

Gaines was fuming but he forced himself to speak lower. "Listen, Tom. I want you to listen to me. Are you listening?"

"Sure," I said.

"Good. Sharina will close your charts and I'll see your patients—the ones that show up, that is. You can do the transfer yourself and once it's done, which shouldn't take you more than an hour, I want you to report to my office. Understood?"

"And Sharina will do all the intakes, as well as close her charts and mine?" This I found insane, since Sharina was an especially slow worker and could barely cover half of what I usually did.

"That's right."

A Loud Humming Sound Came From Above

"Alrighty, then." I said.

In an unsettled state, I began to make the calls and do the paperwork for the client's temporary transfer. About an hour later, after a number of mistakes, since I had trouble keeping my mind on the work, I finished and faxed off the final documents. Now what to do? I thought, feeling miserable. Then it dawned on me. I would become sick, and would have to go home and take a partial sick day. I had never used any sick time, so I knew I couldn't be challenged. I called Gaines and told him I was feeling very ill and would have to go home. There was no response for a moment and I finally said, "Hello? Are you still there?"

"Tom...I'm..." I was sure he was looking up my sick days on his computer and seeing that I'd never taken any. "Make sure you fill out a pink slip and clock out before you leave," he said in a quiet, strange voice, then hung up. I gathered my stuff and headed out for the day. It felt good walking down the street a free man, but I also felt that my time as a counselor was probably running out. Gaines was most likely already in Caldwell's office, ranting and raging. And Tuesday, I would surely be pulled in.

I actually entertained the thought of buying some dope, since it would have totally calmed me down. But I knew I'd initially get sick, because I was so clean, and it wouldn't be until the second day that I'd actually start to enjoy it. I'd need another day to get over a slight jones, or at least a dull yearning. And it would only set me up for doing it again the following weekend. Soon enough, I'd be chipping once, twice a week. And...well, it was just too dangerous, so I chased

The Methadone Clinic

the thought away.

Monday, I slept late and awoke with a hangover that took the rest of the day to get rid of. It was a holiday, and I hated holidays since most places were closed. I was already getting nervous about the confrontation that would surely occur the next day. Even though the weather had turned cold and unpleasant, I decided to go for a walk.

I was walking with no real destination in mind when I noticed I was approaching an area of adult bookstores, rundown bars, rooming houses, massage parlors, and a garishly lit liquor store. Then I saw Robert Gaines. I stepped behind a parked van and watched as he took a furtive look around before ducking into one of the massage parlors. Was this some kind of magic moment? I felt I had to do something—what, I didn't know. If I could somehow document this...a photo? I went into the liquor store and pointed to the cheapest disposable camera I saw. I stood under the glaring lights to read the instructions and took a couple of shots of a vacant lot across the street. I stuck it into my pocket and made my way to the massage parlor. Was this crazy? So what if I had a picture of him getting a massage? But I suspected he was going in there for more. But a picture? I'd have to peek in all the rooms. And surely there'd be security and photographs would be forbidden.

I was buzzed in; they were probably watching me on a monitor. At the top of a narrow stairway, three not-unattractive Asian girls were in a room that was bare except for a tattered easy chair, a wall phone, and a crooked, marked-up wall calendar that showed

A Loud Humming Sound Came From Above

a black pug sitting on a white cushion for October.

"What can we do for you?"

"Er...how much is a massage?"

As the others giggled, one said, "How much you pay?" But another answered, "Fifty dollars, or seventy-five for full." What was I thinking? I didn't have that kind of money to spend. Well, I'd come this far. "Okay, fifty," I said. One took me by the hand and led me through a door, down a semi-dark hallway. We passed a series of rooms, all with long curtains at the portals. I heard low voices, some grunts, squishy sounds, and a radio playing jazz. Then I heard his voice.

The girl was trying to pull me away as I was feeling for my camera. "I wanna listen," I whispered, "Here, extra money...a couple of minutes." I shoved some money at her and shooed her. Reluctantly, she stepped away and pointed to another room, pulling back the curtain before going in. I figured she'd call security, but I got out the camera and stepped into the room, which was, oddly, fairly well-lit. There before me was a surprised, then angry, Robert Gaines, his pants around his ankles. A girl was on her knees with his cock in her mouth. I managed to take two shots before Gaines tried a lunge, falling into the kneeling girl who screamed. Moving quickly back down the hallway, I heard loud voices and activity. I passed a girl sprawled in the easy chair talking on a cell phone. I hurried down the steps and reached the door. Outside, another Asian girl, smoking a cigarette, looked at me a little startled. I walked down the block, turned a corner, crisscrossed, took a bus to some neighborhood where I'd never been, and finally, another bus back. I was up most of the night, but eventually I took a couple of

The Methadone Clinic

Valium and got to sleep.

In the morning, deciding to squeeze Robert Gaines a little more, I called in sick early, leaving a pained phone message.

The following day, I showed up bright and energized, and said a warm hello to everyone, including an expressionless Gaines who said, "Giles. In my office now please."

Despite the "please," I was half-expecting a physical attack. I insisted that he enter the office first. He went in and sat down at his desk.

"Shut the door, please."

I did, but remained standing.

"Okay, how much do you want?" he asked, looking down at his lap.

"Really, I only want to be left alone."

There followed an unnerving silence.

Robert Gaines's visage began changing before me; his facial muscles tightened then slackened, and his eyes seemed to glaze over. His pallor turned gray, and he turned on a very creepy smile.

"Okay," he said in a low voice. "It's a deal."

"Well, there is one other thing," I said, shifting my weight to one leg. He looked at me cautiously. "You know those bonuses everyone's been talking about?"

Gaines coughed and looked away. "Alright, you'll get one of those, too. Now, please, I have a lot of work to do."

As I left his office, a surge of joy came over me, as though some dark yet benevolent angel had sprinkled me with a magical dust, and the residue of that good feeling remained with me for the entire day.

RUDOS AND RUBES PUBLISHING

Rudos and Rubes Publishing is dedicated to making available worthwhile fiction and non-fiction works, an admittedly unusual activity in the modern publishing industry. Our editorial staff consists of unrepentantly dilettante bibliophiles with no interest in searching for the lowest common denominator of public taste.

Information on other Rudos and Rubes releases appears on the following pages. Further information may be obtained by those with Internet access at:

www.rudosandrubes.com

THE GUILT OF THE TEMPLARS
by G. Legman

"...deeply erudite and highly entertaining... sometimes malicious, occasionally replulsive..."
-*The New York Review of Books*

Because so much nonsense concerning the Order of Knights Templars has been promulgated in recent fiction (some of it unfortunately passed off as fact), it seemed proper to make available this fascinating, long out of print interpretation of the Templars' guilt.

Charged with heresy, sacrilege, blasphemy, and sexual perversion, the Templars were summarily arrested, tried, burned at the stake, and their Order extinguished in 1312. Whether the suppression of the Order was justified, and whether the Templars were guilty or innocent, are questions that continue to stimulate the minds of those interested in the intellectual development of Western civilization.

The Guilt of the Templars is one of the rarest works of the late Gershon Legman (1917-1999), bibliographer for the Kinsey Institute and author of *Rationale of the Dirty Joke* and *Love & Death*. Prof. Bruce Jackson termed Legman "the person, more than any other, who made research into erotic folklore and erotic verbal behavior academically respectable."

Drawing on the actual depositions and confessions of the Templars, and probing deeper than the religious, financial, or political issues, Mr. Legman's searching analysis of the effects of suppressing normal sexuality remains a unique and brilliant interpretation of the nature of the Templars' guilt.

DEVIL BORN WITHOUT HORNS
by Michael A. Lucas

Specimens of modern day crime fiction generally fall squarely into one of two categories: dull "whodunits" that might more properly be labeled "who cares whodunits" or half-baked exercises in hard-boiled attitude.

In a field so overrun with generic output, we are tempted to call *Devil Born Without Horns* a breath of fresh air except that it might imply a sweetness and light that is studiously avoided in this darkly humorous, at times brutal, tale of crime and conspicuous consumption in the high-end furniture industry.

"Although I'd often been told that a college education would prove useful regardless of whatever else I did in my life, my bachelor's degree was of no help whatsoever in making up my mind to shoot someone. . . . Despite a lack of suitable academic preparation, I was able to make my decision in time to cripple a running target from nearly twenty feet away—not too bad, I think."

www.rudosandrubes.com

RAW RUMBLES! THE HAL ELLSON OMNIBUS: DUKE/TOMBOY/THE KNIFE

We are proud to present this long-overdue collection of three classic, out of print, "juvenile delinquent" novels by the dean of the field, Hal Ellson (1910-2000). Although many self-appointed moral guardians were outraged when his work originally appeared, more experienced authorities knew that Ellson's vivid depictions of urban violence and despair were all too accurate.

As Dr. Frederic Wertham wrote in the *American Journal of Psychotherapy*: "... it is a surprise to come across so excellent a book as *Duke*. . . . Such a book depends of course on one thing, namely truth—the authentic truth of real conditions, the psychological truth of individual reactions, the artistic truth of presentation, and the moral truth of facing evil that exists right under our noses."

"Hal Ellson rips aside the words 'juvenile delinquency' and shows the horror and tragedy beneath. He takes the whole shocking and brutal story and flings it down as a challenge!"
  -*Christian Science Monitor*

www.rudosandrubes.com

GOSPEL OF DIRT
by B.H. Harvey

This is the book that finally nails shut the coffin of the hard-boiled private detective novel. Penned pseudonymously by a practicing private investigator whose well-earned contempt for the clichés of private eye fiction is evident in the rather sadistic pleasure he takes in pummeling them, *Gospel of Dirt* revitalizes the effete notion of genre deconstruction by pushing it into the realm of genre destruction.

"I opened the door, and walked inside to the familiar smell. I'd missed it. I felt beat up, which, after being beat up, was a quite natural way to feel, although my pocket full of painkillers lifted my spirits some. It was comforting to see the welcome mat to my place, a black rubber job with "IRREGULAR" printed on it via stencil and spray paint. I had a big taped bandage on my belly that made noises whenever I shifted. I shifted a lot. I was on edge. Antsy. Itching to move with nowhere to go. I checked my phone. There were no messages. My bills were still overdue. I hadn't had a case in a month. I sat in my office beat to shit and a half step up from broke, and waited for human misery to come through my door. It just wasn't selling that November."

www.rudosandrubes.com